CASTLE SPELLBOUND

John DeChancie

ACE BOOKS, NEW YORK

This book is an Ace original edition,
and has never been previously published.

CASTLE SPELLBOUND

An Ace Book / published by arrangement with
the author

PRINTING HISTORY
Ace edition / November 1992

ISBN: 0-441-09407-4

Ace Books are published by The Berkley Publishing Group,
200 Madison Avenue, New York, New York 10016.
The name "ACE" and the "A" logo
are trademarks belonging to Charter Communications, Inc.

PRINTED IN THE UNITED STATES OF AMERICA

10 9 8 7 6 5 4 3 2 1

This book is dedicated to
Ann Cecil, Barb Carlson,
Kevin, Charlene, and Sasha Riley,
Glenn Chambers, Mary Tabasko, Deborah Ayres,
Don Cox, Erin Kelly, Jim Lutton,
Matt Urick, Jeff Nartic, Janet Staples,
Nancy Janda, Lara VanWinkle,
Don Turner, Randy Hoffman and all the members
of the Pittsburgh Area Realtime
Scientifiction Enthusiasts' Club,
affectionately known as PARSEC.

"Fairy fair, Fairy fair, wish thou me well;
'Gainst evil witcheries weave me a spell!"

—Nora Archibald Smith (1859–1934)

CASTLE SPELLBOUND

OUR STORY BEGINS

ONCE UPON A TIME, in a great enchanted castle far, far away, there lived two apprentice magicians, Thorsby and Fetchen by name.

They liked to party.

Drinking and wenching were their chief avocations, magic being merely something they had to do to earn their keep. Mediocre sorcerers, they were quite adept at procrastination. In fact, at the craft of inventing excuses to take longer than was necessary to accomplish their appointed tasks, and in the fine art of goldbricking in general, they were past masters.

And they were continually being called on the carpet for it.

"Miserable wastrels!"

Thorsby looked up from his gin rummy hand. "Sorry, Spellmaster. What was it you said?"

"Stand to attention!"

Thorsby and Fetchen shot to their feet. Cards fluttered to the oaken floor.

"Turn around!"

Spellmaster Grosmond clasped his hands behind his back and paced back and forth in front of them, dressing them up and down with dark, close-set hawk's-eyes. He didn't like what he saw.

He stopped before Thorsby, bringing his nose to within an inch of the apprentice's.

"Were you or were you not supposed to look after the ventilation spell in the east wing of the keep?"

"I was, sir."

"And did you?"

"I . . . I'm afraid I haven't got to it quite yet, sir."

"Not quite yet. I see. And might I ask when you'll be troubling yourself?"

"Uh, immediately, sir. I was just going to get to it after break."

"Ah, you're on break, are you?"

"Yes, sir."

"Both of you?"

"Yes, sir," Fetchen confirmed.

"Correct me if I'm wrong, but haven't you two been on break all morning?"

"No, sir!" they piped.

"I swear I walked past this ready room just after breakfast and saw the two of you fiddling with pasteboard, just as now."

"Sir, couldn't have been us," Thorsby suggested.

"I suppose not. My mistake."

Stroking his gray beard, Grosmond sidestepped to Fetchen.

"Am I again mistaken or did I see a report about flies in the Queen's Dining Hall on this morning's task sheet?"

"You did, sir."

"And did you, Master Fetchen, as Pest-Remover-on-Watch, go to the Queen's Dining Hall and find flies?"

"Yes, sir. Swarms of them. How they got there is anyone's guess."

"I could venture one. They came through a nearby outdoor portal, caught the scent of food, and went directly thence. Sound plausible to you?"

"Rather plausible at that, sir."

"So let me ask you this, Master Fetchen. Why are there still swarms of flies—nay, a blizzard of them, buzzing madly about—in the Queen's Dining Hall?"

"Sir, they didn't respond to the usual fly-shooing spell."

"Oh, they didn't?"

"No, sir. These appear not to be your ordinary run of fly."

"Not your ordinary run of fly. I see, I see. And when the fly-shooing enchantment didn't work, what did you do?"

"Well, nothing for the moment, Spellmaster, except to seek out Journeyman Quesnor and solicit advice."

"And what advice did Journeyman Quesnor have for you?"

"None, sir. I couldn't find him."

"And?"

"'And,' sir? Well, I didn't quite know what to do then, sir."

"Oh, you didn't?"

"Uh . . . no, sir."

"I see. So you did nothing, and the king's Guests had no breakfast this morning."

"Well, there was nothing I could have done about it, sir."

"Nothing. And here you sit, playing gin."

"Uh . . . well, sir. You see, it's like this—"

"*Shut that jabbering hole of yours!*"

"Yes, sir."

Grosmond continued pacing, his long black robes sweeping the crumb-littered floor.

"This place is a sty," he grumbled. "Did it ever occur to

any one of you apprentices to take a whisk broom—? Ah, never mind.''

He whirled on the two of them.

''Mark my words. I've had my eye on the twain of you. You're alike, two peas in a pod. Whenever trouble arises, somehow you two turn up at the bottom of it.''

Thorsby said, ''Sir, you really oughtn't—''

''Silence!''

Grosmond folded his arms and tapped his right toe. ''I've had enough of your lollygagging and a bellyful of your endlessly inventive excuses. You two will either shape up or be sacked from the apprentice program.''

Fetchen piped, ''You may rest assured we'll do the former, sir!''

''Oh, may I? I'm not at all sure. Well, we'll see. Meanwhile, I'm taking you off regular day shift and putting you on special detail.''

Thorsby ventured, ''May I ask, Spellmaster, what special detail?''

''You may. Recently an ancient storage room was discovered in the cellar of the King's Tower. Hadn't been entered in years. No dust spell, or the one that'd been laid on long ago had fizzled. Consequently, the place is a mess. Have you heard of this?''

''Uh, yes, sir,'' Fetchen said. ''They say there's many a curious artifact down there.''

''Yes, possibly quite a number of historical value, once the Chamberlain can get in there to sort things out. But he can't until the place is cleaned up.''

''A dust-vanishing spell will do the trick, sir,'' Thorsby offered. ''We can do those right well, sir.''

''No vanishing spells!'' Grosmond warned. ''You might magick something of value into oblivion. No, lads. Elbow grease will be your philtre, a broom your only talisman.''

"Really, sir," Fetchen protested weakly.

Grosmond drew menacingly close to him. "Do I hear an objection?"

Fetchen swallowed. "None, Spellmaster Grosmond."

Grosmond smiled sweetly. "I thought not."

He turned and began walking out of the ready room.

"Get down there now, and be quick about it!" he growled over his shoulder.

"Yes, sir!" the two chorused.

When Grosmond's footsteps faded, Thorsby called out, "Ready—salute!"

Thumbs came up sharply to meet noses.

They laughed.

"The old fart's losing it. He really didn't remember it was us this morning."

"And mostly every morning," Thorsby guffawed. He yawned and looked at the clock. "Lunchtime, almost."

"Let's get down there and start," Fetchen said. "Or Grosmond'll roast our arses. We'll stop by the kitchen and pick up grub."

"Capital idea. And a bottle of something, too."

They sauntered out of the room, leaving their gin hands to decorate the floorboards.

SHEILA'S WORLD

"TRENT? WAKE UP, DEAR."

He opened his eyes to a bright blue sky. The sun was low; it was late afternoon. A soft salt breeze blew in from the ocean.

"Huh?"

Sheila, his wife, was bending over him, hand on his shoulder. "You were moaning. Having a bad dream?"

He sat up on the chaise longue. Before him lay the aquamarine expanse of the hotel swimming pool, placid in the declining tropical sun. The shadows of palm trees crossed its deep end.

He rubbed his eyes, then yawned.

"Are you okay?" she asked him.

"Yeah, sure. Just a dream."

"Bad one?"

"Don't quite remember. Weird . . . just weird."

He looked at Sheila. She was tall, red-haired and beautiful, and he loved every inch of her. He surveyed her up and down, as if for the first time. She was quite fetching, especially in this colorful, delightfully translucent silk frock.

"Our guests are going to arrive any minute," she said.

"Guests?" He had a sense that he'd been away for some time. The dream . . .

"Our cocktail party for Incarnadine's birthday? He didn't want a fuss made, so we're throwing him a little shindig by the pool. Remember?"

"Oh. Yeah. Sure, sure. Is Inky here yet?"

"Not yet," Sheila said, turning. "But here's Gene and Linda."

"Yo, dudes!" Gene called. "And dudesses."

"Hello!" Sheila went to greet the first of her guests.

Trent yawned again. "Man, I gotta stop eating those submarine sandwiches so late at night."

He shucked his terrycloth shirt and walked to the deep end of the pool. Mounting the diving board, he walked to its far extremity and bounced up and down a few times, then took a few steps back. After a moment's mental preparation, he took three even strides, jumped, and dove, his body straight and true, his trajectory a perfect arch. He cut the surface cleanly, with minimum splashing, like a thrown spear.

The cool chlorinated water washed the sleep from him. He stayed submerged, relishing the hushed drone of underwater sounds and exploring the pool's bubbling blue-green depths.

Not much down here. Bare concrete below; a drain. He gave some thought to going snorkeling soon, or at least taking the glass-bottomed tour boat out to explore the local marine life, plentiful in this world of mostly ocean. He had always had a passing interest in marine biology.

Then again . . . to hell with it.

Of late he had found it increasingly difficult to work up

enthusiasm for much of anything. Maybe it was his job. He ran Club Sheila, which in any other world would have entailed bossing the staff, booking blocks of rooms and function space for tours and conventions, keeping the books, placating irate guests, and performing the hundreds of other duties that the job of running a major resort would require. But this world was different. The hotel, the pool, the cabanas, even most of the guests, were phantasms. Magical constructs conjured out of the occult ether by his wife, a powerful sorceress. The place really needed no looking after. How it all worked was beyond him. He himself—a magician of no mean talents—had never worked conjuring magic on such a scale.

Yet, here it was. Club Sheila. SheilaWorld. Real, down to its inscribed ashtrays and custom matchbooks; real unto the satin sheets and the tiny complimentary bars of beauty soap in the hotel's luxurious marble bathrooms.

Real down to the very swimming pool in which he was running out of breath. He angled toward the surface.

He broke water to the sound of laughter and clinking glasses. The staff had set up tables and a portable bar at the other end of the pool. A few more guests had arrived. Trent did a slow dog paddle to the edge of the pool.

"What are you drinking?" Cleve Dalton asked Lord Peter Thaxton.

"Something called a Samoan Fogcutter."

"Sounds potent. What's in it?"

"Rum and a hodgepodge of sweet stuff." Lord Peter wrinkled his nose. "Don't like drinks with little umbrellas and things in them."

"This is good."

"That? What is it?"

"Mai Tai. Rum, grenadine, and a bunch of juices."

"Heavy on the rum today, eh? Well, I'll have one of these and then switch to Scots whisky neat."

"A purist."

More guests arrived, and more exotic drinks were made and handed out. Food lay heaped on a nearby table, the theme Polynesian: pineapple and roast pig and fire-baked fish and steamed seafood and tropical fruit in dozens of dishes.

"What kind of drink is that?" Linda asked Melanie McDaniel. "Looks strange."

"A Blue Lagoon," freckle-faced Melanie told her. "I asked for something really different, and I got something blue."

"What's in it?"

"I don't know."

The bartender—a thin young man who looked a bit like a young Elisha Cooke, Jr.—said, "Blue curaçao, ma'am, along with Triple Sec, vodka, and pineapple juice."

"Tastes pretty good," Melanie said after taking a sip.

Gene Ferraro sidled over and put his arm around Melanie's thinning waist (she'd had twins not long ago). "Drink four of those and come up see my etchings."

She bumped him away with her hip. "You old tease. You talk a great line but you never deliver."

"Why, that's not true. I used to have a paper route."

"Phooey."

Linda said, "Gene leads his love life outside the castle."

"Yeah, I'm a regular Don Juan in the real world. Here I can't get arrested."

"I'll arrest you," Melanie offered.

"Oooh, with handcuffs? Now who's teasing?"

Melanie giggled. Linda motioned toward Gene's drink. "What's that?"

"Iced Tea."

"You on the wagon?"

"It's a drink. Rum, vodka, gin, Triple Sec, sour mix . . . and, uh . . ."

"Orange juice and cola, sir," the bartender supplied.

"Right."

"Heavens, that sounds dangerous," Linda said, wide-eyed. "Rum and vodka and *gin*?"

"Oh, my."

"His Majesty, the king!"

All eyes swiveled to the French doors on the patio. Through them strode Incarnadine, Lord of the Western Pale, and by the grace of the gods, King of the Realms Perilous. His yellow T-shirt bore magenta lettering that read: DEATH'S A BITCH—THEN YOU'RE REINCARNATED. He wore mirror shades, electric-green Bermudas, pink-accented LA Gears, and a big Panama hat with a purple hatband.

"Hey, gang, I'm ready to howl."

Women curtsied, men bowed.

"Tut, tut." He waved his indulgence. "Where can I get a drink? Oh, there." He went straight to the bar.

"What will it be, Your Majesty?"

"Ahhh . . . recommend something."

"Planter's Punch?"

"Nah."

"Rum Runner?"

"Nope."

"Perhaps a Kamikaze?"

"What's in it?"

"Vodka, gin, sake, peach schnapps, and lime juice."

"Sounds suicidal, all right. Can you make an Alabama Slammer?"

"Uh, Southern Comfort, orange juice . . . and—?"

"Amaretto and sloe gin."

"Right, sir. Yes, sir, coming right up."

The king turned his head. "Trent!"

His brother stepped up to the bar. Incarnadine took his outstretched hand.

"Your Majesty. Happy birthday."

"Thank you muchly. Sheila! Long time no see."

"Welcome!" Sheila said as she gave the king a hug. "You haven't been here in so long!"

"The press of business. I do need a vacation. Maybe I'll stay on a few days."

"The royal suite is always ready."

"Some deep-sea fishing, maybe."

"We have a fleet of boats that sits around."

"There's a funny kind of, sort of, marlin out there," Trent told him. "A real terror to land."

"Oh? sounds interesting."

"Poisonous spines."

"Sounds like fun."

"I'll take you out."

"It's a date. Tomorrow."

"Great," Trent said. "How's Zafra and the kids?"

"Wonderful, wonderful. You two seem to be doing fine. All sun-bronzed and healthy."

"Oh, this climate agrees with me, all right," Sheila said, "but I still get burned a lot. Even my spells don't keep the sun off."

Squinting one eye, Incarnadine held up his right hand and slowly waved two fingers. "Hmmm. Strange magic."

"Only Sheila's been able to deal with it so far," Trent said. "I have a devil of a time."

"I suspect I would, too. But maybe a simple forfending spell would take care of the sunburn?"

"Tried it," Sheila said. "It kept up a shield all right, but it kept air out, too."

"Hardly practical. Let me see . . ."

"It's tricky, Inky."

Incarnadine nodded. "I see what you mean. Spells here tend to have unexpected consequences."

"All spells spin off unwanted side-effects," Trent said, "but here they sometimes run rampant."

"Take this hotel, for instance," Sheila said. "All I wanted to conjure was a hut. And look what I got."

The three of them took in the rococo elegance of Hotel Sheila.

"Remarkable," Incarnadine said. "I don't think I could do as good a job."

"It's not me, it's the magic here."

"It's you," Trent assured her. "You're a sorceress of the first magnitude."

"Well, maybe here I am."

Incarnadine asked, "What've you been up to, Trent?"

Trent accepted a Singapore Sling from one of the bartenders and shrugged. "Not much. Just running this place."

"Like it?"

"Like it fine."

"Don't have a hankering to get back to Earth?"

Trent shook his head. "No. Still have the estate on Long Island, but I've put it in mothballs, pretty much."

"Going to retire here?"

"Hell, I'm only three hundred forty-six years old. Give me a break."

Sheila rolled her eyes. "*Only* three hundred forty-six, he says. And he doesn't look a day over forty."

"Really?" Trent said, feigning pique. "And here I'd thought I could pass for thirty-five on a good day."

"A young forty," Sheila amended.

Incarnadine persisted. "So what do you want to do with

the rest of your allotted three score years and five hundred?''

Trent jerked one shoulder. ''Who knows. I'll find something to arouse my interest.''

''Want to fight a war?''

''Eh?''

''I'm serious, I've got two on my hands. And although I could contrive, by magical means, of course, to be two places at once, you can't really divide your attentions that way. I need a good strategist, and you're one of the best I know of.''

''I don't think I like this,'' Sheila said.

Incarnadine laid a reassuring hand on her shoulder. ''Don't worry, my dear. He'll be well behind the front lines. In fact, he can do all his operational planning here and messenger orders to the front, through the castle. He'll be quiet safe.''

''Oh,'' Sheila said. ''Well, in that case . . .''

''In other words, I wouldn't have actual command,'' Trent said.

''I need a plan for a lightning offensive. I want to get the war over quick, very quick. Minimum casualties.''

''What's the milieu?''

''Late Bronze Age.''

Trent laughed. ''Good luck. And here I was thinking laser-guided missiles.''

''I'm of a mind that it can be done at any level of technological development.''

''Well, I'm of a mind to agree with you, but the strategic situation has to be just right.''

''This one is near perfect. We have naval superiority, slightly superior numbers, and better-trained soldiers.''

Trent asked, ''Then why do you need me, particularly?''

''As I said, I want minimum casualties. What this world

lacks is superior military science. Things are fairly primitive on that score. Wars tend to be long and bloody. I want this one to be short and, while I can't hope for zero casualties, I want the body count to be as low as possible."

Trent nodded. "Gotcha. What's the mission objective?"

"Reducing a fortified town near the sea. You won't be able to lay siege immediately, though, because they can field a pretty good army. Once you reduce their numbers, they'll use the town as a redoubt. . . ." Incarnadine smiled. "Do I detect a note of interest?"

Trent half-smiled. "Perhaps you do."

"Well, let's delay the briefing. This is a party, no shoptalk allowed."

"I still don't quite like the idea of Trent fighting a war," Sheila said.

"More like a war game," Trent remarked, "judging from the sound of it. At least it'll be such to me, sitting in my den with maps and unit markers."

"Still . . ." Sheila remained unconvinced.

"Think it over," Incarnadine said. "Let me know. We have some time in that theater. In the other one, things are a bit more critical."

"Oh? What's the milieu there?"

"Muskets and cavalry charges."

"Sounds more like my line of work."

"Sorry, that one I have to handle myself. Still interested?"

Trent took a long drink, then said, "Yes. Yes, I think I am."

"I'll have my operational staff brief you in the morning. Okay?"

"Okay. And thanks, Inky."

"You look like you need something to get the blood rushing. Besides, you're getting a paunch."

Sheila shook her head. "You two keep talking as though he's going to be fighting this war."

Trent pulled his wife closer. "Woman, you are not to worry, hear? This is strictly a desk job. Right, Inky?"

"Right."

"Though I might have to pay a few visits to this world to get the feel of things," Trent dissembled.

"He won't have to go anywhere near the actual fracas," Incarnadine lied blackly.

"Right."

"Well, okay," Sheila said dubiously.

A band struck up a Caribbean beat. Couples took to dancing.

"Let's dance," Sheila said, dragging her husband away.

"Sure. See you later, Inky."

"Have a good time."

The king slurped up the last of his Slammer and turned back to the bar.

"I think I will try a Kamikaze."

"You're quite sure, my liege lord?"

"*Banzai!*"

KING'S TOWER—CELLAR

THORSBY TOOK ANOTHER PULL on the bottle of cooking sherry and put a foot up on the old carved table at which he sat. He belched loudly.

Not far away, Fetchen swept the floor desultorily, pushing dust back and forth.

"You missed a spot," Thorsby told him, pointing.

"Up yours," Fetchen said pleasantly.

Thorsby laughed. Then he yawned. "I never seem to get enough sleep," he complained. "Think I might bed down on that old settee over there, catch a wink."

"You could sweep just a little."

Thorsby looked around. "Well, there's only one broom, isn't there?"

"Now that's a fix." Fetchen threw the broom at him.

Grinning, Thorsby caught it neatly and laid it aside.

"Sit down," he said. "Take a load off."

Fetchen came over and snagged the bottle from him. "You've just about drunk the whole bloody thing."

"Wasn't much left."

Fetchen guzzled the dregs of the sherry and tossed the bottle among some heaped rags and boxes in a corner.

"Look at him making a filthy mess."

Fetchen glanced around at the piles of crates, stacks of musty books, battered antique furniture, and other junk. "What are you puling about?"

Thorsby belched again. Then he farted.

"First intelligent comment we've had out of you all day."

"Shut your hole. I need a drink."

"That sherry's bleeding awful."

"Yes, quite. Let's conjure something."

"You do awful stuff. Undrinkable."

"Well, it's alcohol, isn't it?"

"Marsh water."

"You do it, then."

Fetchen scowled.

Thorsby chuckled. "Not so easy, eh? Food magic's hard enough, but drink magic—well, now."

"Wait a minute." Fetchen got up, crossed the crypt, and began rummaging in a pile of debris. "Saw something when I moved this stuff . . . now, where did I—? Oh, here it is."

He returned bearing a tattered leatherbound book, which he set on the table in front of Thorsby. "Have a look at that."

"An old grimoire," Thorsby said after glancing at it. "So?"

"Read the title."

Thorsby wiped the dust away. "*The Delights of the Flesh.*" He sat up. "Ye gods."

"There's one the Royal Librarian keeps under lock and key."

"I should say so." Thorsby opened the book and began leafing through it.

Fetchen moved his chair. "Oh, look at her."

"A houri."

"Ah. Two of them."

"Imagine being crushed between two sets of—"

"Gods, look at *that* one."

"They have names. Fatima . . . Jalila . . . Layla . . . Safa—"

"Who cares a fig for their names?"

"And here are the spells to conjure 'em with."

"Dare we? I remember warnings about this book."

"Can you resist *that*?"

Fetchen slavered at the full-page engraving. "Not for long."

Thorsby flipped more pages. "There's everything here. Food spells, love charms, all manner of opiates and philtres—"

"Drink. Let's have a drink."

"All right, then. Where's the incantation?"

"No, you have to do the thing in the front of the book first. The general invocation and pact."

"Exactly who and what are we invoking? What kind of magic is this?"

"It's ancient, and very tricky."

"Not the sort of stuff you learn in school, is it?"

"It's on the Index of Proscribed Books. I remember it."

"Who cares. We can handle it."

Fetchen made a dubious face.

Thorsby winked. "Come on, then. Just a few of the more innocuous spells. Can't hurt, can it?"

"I dunno."

"Are you game or are you not, Fetchen?"

Fetchen thought about it, then replied, "I'm game."

* * *

It took a good hour to clear away debris, sweep the floor clean, and inscribe magical symbols on it. The pattern was a set of interlocking geometric figures. None were traditional pentacles.

"Odd," Thorsby opined.

"That's it, then. All done."

"What now? Incantations?"

"None. 'Upon the completion of these devices, the pact is sealed thereon.'" Fetchen threw the book down. "Now we get everything we wish for."

"Just like that?"

"Just like that."

"All right, then. Give us a bottle of wine."

A bottle appeared in the air not far from Thorsby's head, hung for a split second, then dropped.

Delighted, Thorsby caught it. "That's the ticket! Oh, look, it's bubbly."

"Let's have two bottles," Fetchen said, and another instantly appeared.

Thorsby worked the cork up on his and popped it. He upended the bottle and drank deeply. Swallowing, he regarded his partner with a look of disbelief. "That's . . . it's delicious! I've never—"

Fetchen drank from his. "It can't be just wine."

"Ambrosia!"

"The nectar of the gods!"

"Let's have more!" Thorsby commanded. "And food. Lots of food. A kingly feast!"

"And the women to serve us."

"Gods yes, the women," Thorsby said, rushing to the discarded book. He picked it up and frantically paged.

"This one . . . and this one. Oh, can't forget her."

"For you? Three?"

"Why not? You can have four if you want. Five."

"Three's all I can handle. Until I get drunk."

"Wait."

Fetchen stopped short of another swig. "What?"

"Grosmond. We have to get this room done."

"Look under 'slaves, menial.' "

"Oh." Thorsby flipped a few pages. "Slaves, factotums. Yes, we need a grunt to do our work. Gods, ugly thing."

"Homunculus."

"I suppose we need someone to clean up after us."

"Right. We need it. Give us this one."

A gnarled, bent form appeared at the center of the conjuring device. It was vaguely manlike, but had an enormous head. One eye was beside the nose, and the one above the nose was smaller, slitlike. The side of its head bulged a bit. One corner of its wide mouth leaked a rivulet of clear fluid. It was short and vaguely male but more androgynous than anything. Its clothing—blue denim bib overalls—lent an incongruous note. Its small four-toed feet were bare.

"Hideous thing," Fetchen said.

"You, there," Thorsby called.

"Yes, master?"

The creature's voice rasped like a saw.

"Take this."

The homunculus stooped to pick up the thrown broom.

"Clean up a bit, will you? There's a good fellow."

"Yes, master. What shall I clean, master?"

"This place."

"All of it, master?"

"Yes, all of it, every last nook and cranny. Straighten it right up. Dust it up good, sort out the junk, and arrange it all on the floor there for inspection. Take care not to cover up the pattern, there."

"Yes, master. Will there be anything else, master?"

"Just do a good job, whatever it takes. And report when you're done."

"Whatever it takes. Very good, master."

The creature began to sweep diligently.

"What now?" Fetchen asked.

Thorsby gulped down more sparkling wine and let out a sigh of supreme satisfaction. He looked at Fetchen with a triumphant grin.

"Now, my friend, we throw a right proper party. The biggest, the best party ever. An orgy. A saturnalia."

Fetchen nodded. He stepped forward to command forces unseen.

"All right, then, let's have your best tits and arse!"

Club Sheila

The sun went down, the tide went out. Everyone began to dance and shout.

"Hey, hey," Gene said, doing the lambada with Linda.

"Ho, ho," Linda averred. She was a good dancer.

"Shake that thing."

They danced lewdly. People watched.

Finally Gene said, "I'm bushed. And this is getting me horny."

"Yeah. Me, too."

"Want to take a walk on the beach?"

"Sure," Linda said.

They walked off the patio and past the pool, into which several people had either fallen, dived, or been pushed. The liquor had been flowing steadily, and things were getting nicely out of hand.

Laughter rang out. The night was festive and gay.

They crossed tennis courts and passed through the fringe of palm trees that edged the beach. Here the water was close, low breakers washing the slowly eroding sand. Linda took her high-heeled shoes off.

They sat together on the beach, legs crossed, knees touching. The moon was directly above, very high, very large, and full. It had dark markings on it that made it look like another planet. Which in fact it was, though a small one. The tides here were strong, much stronger than on Earth. In the morning, when the tide was at its lowest ebb, the surf would recede almost two hundred yards.

"It's a shame to let that romantic moon go to waste," Gene said.

"Sure is," Linda agreed.

She hooked an arm around his neck, drew him close, and kissed him. It wasn't a fooling-around kiss.

They parted and Gene looked at the moon again. "Now, I wonder what brought that on? The booze?"

Linda shrugged. She was a little high. Not all that much, but a little.

"Maybe," she said. "Was I out of line?"

"Not at all. It was just a little surprising. Funny that we've never . . . well, you know."

"Yeah. We're good friends. Buddies."

"That wasn't a buddy kiss."

"Nope. Did you like it?"

"I certainly did."

"Good," Linda said. "Let's do it again."

They did it again, and took their time about it.

"But why now, after all this time?" Gene wanted to know afterward.

"I don't know, Gene. Maybe I never realized how much I like you. Maybe it's about time I stopped waiting for . . ."

"Waiting for Mr. Right?"

"I hate that expression."

"So do I. Maybe it'll take a bit more time."

"I'm tired of waiting."

"But . . ."

She nodded "I know, Gene, I know. Sorry."

"Don't be. I'm not. I think . . . Linda, I think you're carrying a torch for somebody."

"It shows, eh?"

"Yeah. I won't ask who."

"Don't, please." She scooped up some sand. "Oh, hell. I want to tell somebody. But I really can't."

"Then don't."

"But I want to. He's married."

"That's tough."

"Yeah." She tilted her hand to let sand cascade back onto the white beach.

Gene fiddled with a shell some time before asking, "Someone in the castle?"

"Yep."

"Oh. Guest or staff?"

"This is like Twenty Questions. Neither."

"Neither?" Gene was mildly puzzled.

"Oh, forget it. It's hopeless. Never happen. Took me years to realize I was in love with him. Then suddenly I did. I had a dream . . . But as I said, it's hopeless. I should forget. I should get on with my life."

"Such as it is, inside a magical fairy fantasy castle."

Linda giggled. "Magical fantasy fairy castle?"

"Fairly fantastical magic castle."

"Magical fantastical—"

"Faerie castle."

"What?"

"F-a-e-r-i-e castle."

"Oh. How did you pronounce that?"

Gene made a sneering face. "Faeh."

"Faeh?" Linda laughed.

"Faeh-r-r-rie. Faeeeeeerr-r-r-rie."

Linda laughed and fell back onto the sand, stretching her long legs out.

Gene regarded her lithe body. He had never realized what nice legs she had, and her short black cocktail dress made them appear all the more shapely. He had always liked the way she was put together. Why hadn't he ever . . . ?

"Gene?"

"Yes?"

"When I said I was horny I meant it. Don't think you would be second fiddle. I've always thought you were very attractive. You're bright, witty—"

"Gosh and shucks. I like you, too, Linda."

"Don't think . . . Oh, shit. You probably think—everyone probably thinks of me as a cold fish. Asexual."

"Nah."

"Yeah. I know. But it's not that way. I have sexual needs, too."

"Never said you didn't."

"Gene, could we . . . should we have an affair?"

"You know what they say about sex busting up a good friendship."

"Is that what will happen? It doesn't have to, Gene. I won't hold you to anything. Really."

"That's not the issue, Linda. That's not—"

He thought better of saying what he was going to say. He decided to kiss her instead, and bent to the task.

The kiss was interrupted by approaching footsteps. "Here's a jolly spot!" a man's voice said. "Oh, rotten luck. Seems we're intruding on something momentous."

Gene and Linda rolled away from each other and got up.

It was Lord Peter and Cleve Dalton, each with a saronged chambermaid in tow. The women were dark and lovely and smiling.

"Sorry, old chaps," Lord Peter said, waving a bottle

apologetically. "Just in search of a good spot for a moonlight swim."

"No, come ahead," Gene said, with instant regret.

Cleve Dalton began, "We don't want to—"

"Oh, it's only Gene and Linda," Lord Peter scoffed, leading his lady friend out onto the beach.

"I'm going to turn in early," Linda said, picking up her shoes. "I'm bushed."

She gave Gene a long look.

He met her gaze. The matter was somewhere very high up in the air. "Good night," he said.

Linda walked back through the trees. Gene looked after her a long time. He was vexed, puzzled, and unsure.

Presently he turned toward the intruders. Clothes already lay in piles on the beach. The two couples were wading out into the breakers, backlit by the huge moon.

He got a fifth-wheel feeling and began to follow in Linda's footsteps, then halted.

He didn't quite know what he wanted to do.

He struck off down the beach in search of solitude and quiet. And darkness. He had some thinking to do. Some very important thinking.

Why now, he wondered, after all this time?

CELLAR

THE MUSTY OLD CRYPT had gotten somewhat bigger, and in the process had acquired some interesting attributes. Completely transformed, it was now a plush seraglio fit for a sultan, padded with carpets, tapestries, pillows, and rugs. Standing braziers threw off the smoke of fragrant incense. Scented oils burned in dozens of polished silver lamps.

There were two recliners, and on them reclined Thorsby and Fetchen. Attending each were no less than eight houris.

"Peel us a grape, love," Thorsby commanded.

A bare, milky arm reached out, a purple morsel 'twixt thumb and index finger.

"Ye gods, that *is* a peeled grape."

"It is yours but to wish, O Great One," said the houri nearest him.

His hand idly roving across smooth bare female flesh, Thorsby accepted the bit of skinned fruit. It was sweet, melting on his tongue. A burst of flavor filled his mouth, flavor unlike any he had ever experienced.

"Gods, if that's a bloody grape, what's the real food like?"

"Who's hungry?" Fetchen said after ungluing his lips from those of the houri nearest him—one of them, anyway. This said, he attached his mouth to a salient portion of the other's anatomy.

"Yes," Thorsby agreed. "Greater appetites gnaw."

"Why do you delay, Great One?" asked the honey-blond houri.

"Yes, why?" asked the flaxen-haired houri. "Take me again, master!"

"No, take me!" said the one dark of hair and eyes.

"No, me!"

"Me!"

"Ladies, please!" Thorsby sighed. "Demand is greater than supply at the moment. Besides, we don't want to achieve satiety too quickly, now, do we? This way, the expectation is deliciously prolonged."

"You will never achieve satiety, Great One," the brown-haired, green-eyed beauty told him. "Your capacity for pleasure is infinite."

"I was wondering why I was feeling a return of energy so soon after," Thorsby marveled. "You mean—?"

"Yes, Great One. You may indulge every desire, taste every variety of the fruits of passion, and not feel any sapping of strength."

"Bloody wonderful. Well, then . . ."

Thorsby fortified himself from the wine bottle—which, it should be noted, never emptied.

"The same applies to any sense you wish to engage," the redhead informed him. "Taste, touch, hearing, smell—"

"Well, let's see," Thorsby said. "We've got touch pretty well covered. Taste? Yes, let's have some food, finally."

A huge table appeared, laden with a feast fit for the shah of shahs. Dishes were fetched and offered.

"Taste this, Great One."

"This too, Great Sultan!"

"And this!"

"One at time." He nibbled on bread dipped in something. He chewed and swallowed.

"Gods!"

"Does it meet with your approval, Great One? If not, you may order the cook to be boiled in his own oil."

"Ye gods! Fetchen, taste the food!"

Fetchen emptied his mouth. "Wha?"

"Taste this stuff! It's unbelievable."

"Quiet, can't you see I'm feeding?"

"More, O Wonderful Master?"

Thorsby's gaze swiveled back and forth. "I'll try a bit of . . . this. Yes . . . well . . ."

Thorsby ate a cube of spiced meat.

"Merciful gods! That is good! Oh, my heavens. I could eat that all day."

Thorsby began to stuff himself. Between mouthfuls he said, "Fetchen . . . mmph . . . You really must . . . mmph . . . try some of this—"

"Oh, all bloody right." Fetchen grabbed a skewer of barbecued lamb and bit off a chunk. His eyes popped wide. "This is super!"

"Well, I bloody well told you, didn't I?"

Assisted by the houris, Fetchen tore into his food.

"What other senses may we delight, Great and Wonderful Masters?"

Thorsby turned to the honey-blonde. "I can't imagine more. Make some suggestions."

"Why, we have scarcely begun, Great One. Would some entertainment be to your liking as you take your repast?"

"Capital idea!" Thorsby said enthusiastically, his mouth so stuffed he could barely get the words out. "Bring it on, love."

"Do you have preferences, Great One?"

Thorsby swallowed. "Such as?"

"Musicians, singers, tumblers, jugglers—"

"Belly dancers!"

"Your every caprice is law, O Powerful Ruler."

Belly dancers dutifully appeared, with musicians to back them up. They were as beautiful as the other houris and more tempting. They gyrated and shook, bangles jingling, finger-cymbals clashing, to the beat of the tabour and the drone of the doumbek.

"Fantastic!" Thorsby approved.

"And when His Greatness grows weary of them, he needs but to wave a hand and they will go away."

"Never! Bring them on in endless numbers! Let every one be better and more voluptuous than the last. I command it!" Thorsby took another swig of ambrosia. "Right, I'm getting the hang of this."

"We tremble, and obey!" the houris chorused.

"But vary it a bit. Throw in some . . . oh, tap-dancers or something. Chorus lines. Vaudeville acts."

"Your every whim will be obeyed, O Great and Powerful Sultan."

"That's me all over. Isn't it, Fetch, old darling? Fetch? Oh, Fetch?"

Where Fetchen had been, there was now a pileup of nude flesh draped with food.

"Right," Thorsby answered himself.

CASTLE PERILOUS—KEEP

LINDA CAME OUT OF A TROPICAL NIGHT and into the gloom of the castle keep, passing through the portal that linked Sheila's world with Castle Perilous.

It was late afternoon, castle time. An ordinary day. Walking along the hallway, she passed servants and tradesmen going about their appointed tasks, along with a well-dressed nobleman or two about on business. She greeted the people she knew and smiled at those she didn't. She'd often wondered what the total population of the castle was. It must be enormous. She'd been here almost five years, and new faces presented themselves almost every day. To take a census, you'd have to count the population that lived in the various castle "aspects"—the worlds to which the castle provided access—as well as permanent castle residents. And then there were the Guests: people and other beings who had wandered into the castle through any one of 144,000 magical doorways.

The final nose-count would very likely be surprising.

She turned down the hallway that led to her bedroom, still

thinking of Gene and of what had begun to develop between them.

She was now regretting that it had happened; or rather that it only halfway happened. If Dalton and Thaxton hadn't blundered by, something might have, and then the affair would have been a *fait accompli*. Now she had to decide whether she wanted to go through with it. With the alcohol wearing off, she was beginning to see that that would be a tough decision. What would be the mood the next time she and Gene met? What would she say? What would he say?

She didn't relish facing him. Would they simply smile and pretend it didn't happen? Maybe that would be best. Or should they talk it out?

She wondered if Gene was already having second thoughts. Never once in all the time she'd known him did she get the slightest hint that he regarded her as anything but a good friend. A buddy. One of the guys. She had felt no spark, not the faintest throb, in all that time. She began to search her own feelings to see if there was something in her, some tiny glowing coal of desire beneath the sisterly warmth she felt for him.

She would be surprised to find anything.

Maybe . . . maybe she just wanted to get laid.

Well, what was wrong with that? Perfectly natural. She hadn't slept with a man since . . .

She stopped. Good Lord, had it been so long that she couldn't remember?

Was it Tom Fahey, the man she'd been engaged to for three years? No wait. There was the insurance agent—her insurance agent, who had come over to change the beneficiary on her life insurance and ended up asking her out. . . .

Was that after Tom and she had broken up, or before?

During?

Yes, during. It was during the breakup. Yes. She and Tom were just about through when she'd gone out with . . .

She started walking again. What *was* his name? Phil. No, Stu.

Stu Stockton! Yes. Brief fling, that. One of the few, if not the only, brief fling of her life. On the rebound, sort of. Or did it happen before Tom and she got back together for the last time?

She laughed. She was obviously repressing all that. Better left repressed, too. Cover it up, let it lie. The dead past.

Shudder.

So, it had been either Stu or Tom. When? Well, that would have been, oh, almost five and a half, maybe six years ago.

Six years! She didn't believe it. It *couldn't* be six years.

But it was. She couldn't believe she had been non-valent—incapable of bonding—in all that time. Not the slightest urge to pair, not the slightest quiver of desire . . .

Well, not quite. There had been some nights, some cold and lonely castle nights, when she would have liked another warm body in her bed. Not just because Perilous was cold and draughty on occasion. But because she had felt the need to share her feelings with somebody. She had wanted some-one to share a life with, to be a part of someone else's life. She had wanted to touch, to be touched. To sleep with somebody's arm around her.

And, yes, to make love.

She wasn't a cold fish. She wasn't asexual. It was just that she was picky.

Picky, picky, picky, her mother's voice came out of the dark ages of early memory. Eat your dinner, you're not eating. You're getting so thin. Miss Skin-and-Bones! You're too picky, Linda. A fussbudget about food. Too hot, too cold, too sour, too chewy; Linda had always had an excuse not to eat. And she had remained thin and fussy into adulthood. Picky, picky.

And about men, too. Not just anyone would do. In high school she had had few boyfriends. She liked to think she had high ideals. Well, that was true. Maybe too high. Tom had been a wonderful guy, but he was picky, too. More so than Linda. Way too picky. Always judging, always criticizing; first everybody else, then her. She had never measured up to *his* high standards, and she had wearied of the constant sense of failure she had felt.

So maybe high standards were a lot of hooey. Maybe getting laid was just what she needed, for once. Or twice. (Had Stu been just a lay? She barely remembered him. No, there'd been something more to it. Hadn't there?)

Repress, repress.

She reached her bedroom door and grasped the big wrought-iron door handle. The ''lock'' was her own: a magic spell that would admit only her.

Something occurred to her. What if Gene came knocking? What would she do? He might have interpreted her leaving as a signal to meet later. In fact, she had had that in the back of her mind.

Was she afraid of scandal? Afraid for her reputation? She laughed to herself. Did *anybody* care about those things these days? Well, maybe, but they didn't apply in Castle Perilous, at least among Guests. Whatever mores held sway among the native denizens of Perilous, she knew that her fellow Guests wouldn't bat a collective eye at a little bed-sharing. It went on all the time.

What if Gene didn't come? She wondered how she would feel about that eventuality. Rejection? She didn't want that either. Boy, had she opened a can of worms.

Why don't I take a little walk? she thought. Put it off. She left her door and continued down the corridor.

If Gene came home and found her gone he'd probably get upset, even ticked off. Now that she thought of it, that fetching look she'd given him couldn't have been interpreted any other way except as a come-on. So, he comes knocking, expecting, and . . . she's flown the coop. Nothing like leading a guy on and then shutting him off. There were words for the kind of women who made a habit of it. ''Coquette'' was the polite term.

She wouldn't blame him if he did get a little pissed off.

Turning a corner, she came upon the Queen's Dining Hall. Earlier there had been an infestation of flies here. The flies seemed to be gone.

She went on down the hall and made a few turns, two rights and a left, threading her way through the maze of the castle keep. An old castle veteran, she knew her way. She rarely got lost now no matter where she went.

She passed a pretty sitting room, doubled back, and went in. The far wall was cut with six French windows, the extreme right one leading out to a bartizan turret high on the keep that gave a sweeping view of the Plains of Baranthe, some thousand feet below.

The other windows were quite another matter. They looked out onto different worlds altogether: parkland, farmland, forest, plain, and river valley. Nothing spectacular in any; simply pleasant landscapes.

Linda took a seat on the comfortable couch and put her legs up. The situation called for some thinking.

She was distracted by how appealing the room looked. The rug was Oriental, with a design that looked more Indian than Persian. There was a lot of furniture: an ornately carved rolltop desk; a tall, white-lacquered chest of drawers; a walnut trestle table; slat-back chairs; an oaken Gothic stool; several wing chairs; several bookcases holding leather-covered volumes; lots of shelves and dressers displaying ceramic pots, cameo glass vases, bronze statuettes, enamel boxes, silver tankards, and other items of interest.

It was a nice room, cozy. She had run across it before, but it changed every time she encountered it. Which was par for the course in Castle Perilous. Things shifted about helter-skelter on a regular basis, even in the most stable areas of the castle. Sometimes whole rooms relocated themselves, and it was not uncommon for them to disappear entirely, closed off by spontaneously generated blank walls.

They didn't call it Castle Perilous for nothing.

But sometimes the old place was quite homey and comfortable. Linda fluffed am embroidered pillow and sat back.

Getting back to the issue at hand . . .

Gene, Gene, Gene. What did she think of him? Well, he was good-looking, in a way. Dark curly hair; sort of Italian-looking (but didn't he say his mother was Irish?) with regular features, hazel eyes. She liked his face. It was a good face; maybe not what you'd call cute, exactly. Handsome. Yes, Gene was a handsome man. Tall, dark, and handsome. No problem there.

Okay. He was intelligent. Very. Often *too*. He talked well, was quick on verbal feet. Had a penetrating wit. He could make her laugh. Sometimes he was a scream. Some-times he was obscure and made strange comments and you didn't know how to take him; but he always had something pertinent to say. He was good in a fight, that was for sure. He was an excellent swordsman, and he seemed never to be afraid, even in a sticky situation. And together they had found themselves in some very sticky situations.

He was also something of a ladies' man. Women generally liked him. His adventures in other worlds always seemed to involve a romantic liaison or two. The most notorious of these came to light the time he brought back this absolute Amazon of a female out of some bizarre Edgar Rice Burroughs-like universe, a veritable Deejah Thoris, brass brassiere and all. Right off the gaudy cover of a sci-fi paperback. She'd been stunning. But he'd lost her—she'd run off to Earth with some motorcycle types.

There had been other affairs that Linda knew about, both inside the castle and out. Before tonight she had regarded these with a boys-will-be-boys attitude. But now they seemed vaguely threatening.

That was stupid. How could she possibly feel that way? Gene was just a friend. That's all he was.

She sighed. Or was he? *Let's see; add it all up.* Gene was handsome, intelligent, resourceful, trustworthy, loyal, helpful, friendly, courteous, kind, cheerful. . . .

Hey, this guy was Boy Scout of the Year! So why the hell wasn't she head over heels in love with him? What did she want? What was she waiting for?

Kid, you've got to realize that you're no spring chicken anymore. I mean, the big Three-Oh has come and gone; up ahead, the scary Four-Oh, heading right at you.

If not now, when?

Something came into the room. She stared at it before she realized what it was, or rather before realizing that she didn't quite know what kind of creature it was. Her first thought was of a hairless monkey in dungarees, but the head was too large for a monkey's.

Whatever it was, it was humanlike. A gnome? A dwarf? Something like that.

And whatever was it doing sweeping up?

It began its cleanup on the bare part of the stone floor and came toward her.

"Hello," she said as pleasantly as possible. She couldn't tell whether it nodded in response or was just bobbing its bald head, which it constantly did when it moved. She rather thought the latter.

It swept on by her, busy with its straw broom.

One of the servants? she guessed. Was there a new policy to hire the . . . "differently abled"? Well, if so, that was very commendable. She watched it make a quick circuit of the room, marveling at how fast and efficient it—he? she?—was. The longer she watched, the more energy and animation the creature seemed to acquire, until it became a little whirlwind of housecleaning activity. It let go of the broom only to start dusting the shelves with a rag it pulled from its blue bib overalls, carefully lifting every objet d'art to wipe underneath.

It went through the room in no time, leaving the faint odor of cleanliness behind, a whiff of furniture polish, a hint of lemon oil and wax.

When it was done it walked briskly out of the room, moving with a curious bouncing gait, head lolling back and forth. She got up, followed it out, and stood at the arched entrance to watch it go galumphing off down the hall.

"Strangest thing," she said.

It turned a corner and was gone.

"Now, I wonder—"

She heard tiny footsteps behind her, turned, and was amazed to see the same creature heading toward her, broom tucked under its arm. She cast a confused glance back down the corridor. No, it couldn't possibly be the same creature; but this one was absolutely identical to the first, down to the mincing walk and the checkered cloth hanging out of a back pocket.

She watched it go past. It moved purposefully, totally dedicated to its mission, which seemed to be to . . . *clean* things.

At any cost.

CLUB SHEILA

INCARNADINE WAS ON HIS THIRD KAMIKAZE, watching for an opportunity to get Trent alone. A window of opportunity had not presented itself in some time. At the moment Trent was being lionized by a pride of female guests. His Highness had a way with the ladies.

Meanwhile, His Majesty was feeling his liquor, despite a small but usually effective sobering spell. His magic didn't seem to work very well here. No matter, there was time. A little, anyway.

"Your Majesty! How are you tonight?"

He turned to Cleve Dalton. "Cleve! Fine, and you?"

"Chipper, my lord, chipper."

"Getting in any good golf lately?"

Dalton shook his head sadly. "Thaxton's given it up."

"Oh, I'd forgot. But surely you could find another partner?"

"But half the fun was watching his lordship."

Incarnadine laughed. "Yes, I chanced to see him hacking once. Has quite a temper."

"The worst. I do get in an occasional round, but it's not the same."

"Why don't we two go for eighteen sometime?"

Dalton raised his eyebrows, pleasantly surprised. "I'd be honored, sire."

"Though I can't promise any time soon. My schedule's fairly tight at the moment."

"Whensoever it pleaseth His Majesty. I am at your service, good my lord."

Incarnadine smiled. "You're getting pretty good with those Shakespearean turns. Make a habit of that 'good my lord' stuff and you'll be going around in tights and doublet carrying a skull. I've seen it happen to other Guests."

"But where else do I get the chance to use all those ruffles and flourishes? It's fun."

"Have a ball. Listen, I'm going to sidle over and try to talk to my brother. Make a golf date with my secretary and I'll try like hell to keep it. Really I will. And we won't use the public course. I have a private one. It's a little wild but a lot more fun."

"Sounds interesting. Will do, sire."

"See you later."

Incarnadine strolled across the patio. His brother the prince was still at it, bantering volubly. Trent could be garrulous, especially when he was the center of attention. And charming, quite charming.

Old Prince Charming, he of the butter-colored hair and strong jaw. Fine figure of a man, for a former nasty creep who'd caused no end of bother in his time. But no more. Trent had reformed. At least he claimed as much. And Incarnadine believed it. If Trent's recent behavior had been any indication, it was true. He was a changed man. Trent had lent a hand during the dust-up with the Hosts of Hell. Later he'd been kidnapped by them and dumped into this backwater world with Sheila, whom he eventually married. She was of common stock; moreover, she was a castle Guest. The castle nobility had just about written Trent off, but he didn't seem to care; and he did indeed appear to be free of his longtime obsession with seizing the throne, the Siege Perilous.

All true. But it might be good insurance now and then to keep him busy. Hence this little mission. It wouldn't keep him away long.

Just a decade or so.

". . . so the hooker said to the chicken, 'Sure, honey, throw in a jar of mayonnaise and you got yourself a deal.'"

A burst of laughter.

An attendant came up bearing a tray of drinks. "A refill, sire?"

Incarnadine shook his head and set his half-full glass on the tray.

"That was cute," a tall horse-faced woman told Trent. "Filthy, but cute."

"I am nothing if not filthy but cute," Trent said.

She giggled. "Well, I know you're cute. Your filthiness I know only by reputation." She batted her eyelashes.

"Oh, so it's gotten around? I'll have to hire a PR flack to put another spin on it."

"I bet you've given a few women a spin in your time."

"My dear, women are like yo-yos."

"Oh? How so?"

"You let 'em turn at the end of a string for a while, then you snap your wrist and they jump up into the palm of your hand."

"What a charming metaphor."

"Yes, rather."

"That's sexist," someone alleged.

"You mean 'sexy,'" Trent said with an evil smirk.

"You're incorrigible," said the horse-faced woman. "A real throwback. An atavist."

"Attaboy, I always say."

More giggles.

Trent happened to glance Incarnadine's way and did a take. "Your Kinghood! Do join the party."

"I've been watching from afar," Incarnadine said, "making comparisons."

"None invidious, I hope."

"Wilde, Bernard Shaw, and their ilk spring to mind."

"Not exactly the ilk of human kindness, but it's nice to know I'm in stellar company. Thank you, Inky."

"Don't let it go to your head. Might I have a word with you in private, old chum?"

"Certainly, old bean. Ladies, excuse us?"

"Please don't keep him too long, my lord," the woman said. "He's the life of the party."

"And I don't even play the piano," Trent said.

The king led Trent over to the side of the swimming pool, now once again placid and empty of revelers.

"What's up?" Trent asked.

"I know it's short notice, but can you leave tonight?"

"Leave? But I thought you said—"

"I didn't know how to break it to Sheila. There is some urgency. This is a diplomatic mission as well as a military one. You can handle that aspect as well. Can you get away?"

"Well, if it's necessary, yes, I suppose I can leave. It's that urgent?"

"Yes. One thing you have to keep in mind. This world you're going to—"

"Which one is it, by the way?"

"It's called Hellas in the castle worlds list. And the analogues are fairly obvious."

"Never heard of it. Greekish, is it? Well, as long as they don't come bearing gifts."

"Then it's set? You can leave now?"

"Now? Right now?"

"Yes."

Trent shrugged. "Well, I'll have to tell Sheila."

"Yes."

"Uh, I'll make it quick."

"It'd be best."

"Should I tell her how long, approximately?"

"Say a few days."

"Is that true?"

"True enough. Go do it. I'll meet you in the bar."

Trent nodded and went off to find his wife.

Incarnadine crossed the patio and went through wide glass doors into the deserted bar, where he took a booth and fiddled with swizzle sticks for a few minutes until Trent came walking in.

Incarnadine looked up at him. "All set?"

Trent gave a quick nod.

"She's distraught?"

"Not so you'd notice. Let's go."

Incarnadine collapsed his little house of swizzle sticks and got up.

They walked through the bar and out into the spacious lobby, which they crossed to a bank of elevators. One set of doors stood off by itself. These opened. A sign above the doors read CASTLE EXPRESS.

"One thing you have to remember about the universe of Hellas," Incarnadine said as the doors rolled shut.

"What's that?"

"The temporal differential is severe."

The elevator began to descend.

"Oh? How severe?"

"Very. On the order of three hundred to one."

Trent was amazed. "Are you kidding me?"

The king shook his head. "You could stay a year subjective time, but here . . ."

"Nothing. Well, that's fine from Sheila's point of view."

The elevator went down two floors and stopped. Doors set into the back wall of the elevator opened onto a stone-lined corridor lighted by wall-mounted torches that looked like glowing jewels.

They stepped out into the keep of Castle Perilous.

"So you want a quick war," Trent said as they walked the corridor. "Quick and clean, though. Not quick and dirty."

"Yes. If possible."

"Not always possible."

"No, not always. And for 'quick' in this context, read 'relatively quick.' This is an archaic world. Nothing happens quickly but death."

"Right. So, how long, do you figure?"

"That's going to be up to you. There's a fleet assembled from many cities—city-states, really—all over this culture. They've been ready to sail, but there've been political problems. And financial. Squabbles over sharing the costs of the war, etcetera."

"Some things never change."

"You said it. Anyway, the fleet is about ready to sail. But they don't have a rational battle plan. I came up with one, but it will never be followed if I'm not there to hector and cajole. And as I said, I can't be there."

Trent asked, "You want me to follow your game plan?"

"No! I trust you implicitly in this. Your strategy may be better than mine or worse, but it will be yours. You'll have faith in it at least. And you'd change mine, anyway."

"Probably."

"So, that's that. You'll have enough time to size up the strategic situation yourself and come up with a campaign to suit."

"But how much control will I have?"

"You'll have the ear of the commander in chief. The kingpin of the whole operation trusts me implicitly. He's a good leader but is not his world's greatest chess player, if you know what I mean."

"Likes frontal assaults."

"They all do in this world. But this guy knows his limitations—"

"What's the guy's name?"

"Anthaemion. He realizes he's in over his head, and he knows he has to win this one. So he's open to suggestions."

"But will he be open to *my* suggestions?"

"Will he listen to a special emissary, my own brother, a prince of the realm? Sure he will. He doesn't like me being away, but we've talked, and he understands."

"How much does he understand, about Perilous and such matters?"

"The usual cover story. I'm his court magician. I come from a distant foreign land, far, far away. Hyperborea, Shangri-la, *und so weiter.*"

Trent chuckled. "How many potentates play Arthur to your Merlin?"

"Gods! If I had a farthing."

"Okay. By the way, what's the objective? Another city-state, I take it. What's the name of the place?"

"Dardania."

Trent looked thoughtful. "This is beginning to resonate. And what's Anthaemion's outfit called?"

"His city-state? Mykos. The members of the joint military command he heads are generally known as Arkadians, though they don't think of themselves much in that light. This can be a shaky alliance at times."

"Hmm. Let me ask this. What set the whole shooting-match off? What's the war all about?"

"Well, again, the usual thing. They're all pirates in this culture, really. Raid each other constantly, harass the hell out of each other's shipping, and so forth, and it's tolerated to a degree. All's fair, up to a point. But then someone goes too far, breaks an unwritten rule. Then everyone gangs up on the transgressor, and all hell breaks loose."

"But what precipitated it?"

"One gang made off with another gang's women, which is nothing original. They all do it, and worse, but this time the ringleader kidnapped the big king's little brother's wife, and . . . What's the matter?"

Trent had come to a halt, arms folded, regarding Incarnadine with withering skepticism. "Don't tell me. This king's brother's wife. Her name wouldn't happen to be—?"

"It's Alena."

"Ye gods, Inky! What in the name of—"

"The analogues are there, but they're superficial, really."

"Oh, sure."

"No, I'm not kidding. I know it sounds fishy, but—"

"Just a little skirmish, you said. A quick assault. One-two punch and they're out. Right!"

Incarnadine leaned against the smooth stone wall. "Trent, do you want to bow out? No hard feelings if you do."

"Well . . . damn it."

"Seriously, I'll understand."

"So you say now. But you said you were in a bind."

"I'll get by somehow. Don't worry about it."

Scowling, Trent eyed his brother askance.

"It's okay, Trent," Incarnadine said mildly. "Really."

With a deep sigh of resignation, Trent started walking again. "You con artist. You rotten, no-good swindler . . ."

"Really, if you think you can't handle it—"

"Oh, shut up. You know I'm not going to chicken out now."

Watching his brother stalk away, Incarnadine grinned wryly. "I knew I could count on you," he said.

Trent walked resolutely on. "Up yours. Your frigging Majesty."

Incarnadine followed after, his laughter reverberating in the stone corridor.

KEEP—EAST WING,
NEAR THE SOUTHWEST TOWER

KWIP THE THIEF stepped casually along the hallway, whistling tunelessly. He was a small man, preferring his native dress: jerkin, pantaloons, a hat not unlike a beret though larger, and soft black leather boots. He had dark eyes and dark hair and looked to be in his middle years or somewhat younger.

He passed the opening to a smaller side passage and stopped a few feet beyond.

He looked up and down the hallway, his manner still relaxed, perhaps calculatedly so. He listened.

No one about, nobody coming. He walked back to the side passageway, entered it, and covered the short distance to its end, where a stout oak door stood. After a last glance over his shoulder, he reached into a pocket on his jerkin and took out a large skeleton key.

The key was halfway into its hole when he froze. There was something amiss.

He carefully withdrew the key and grasped the door's wrought-iron handle. He pulled gently. The door eased open a few inches. He listened, heard nothing.

He stepped back and quietly drew his sword. Again taking the door handle in his free hand, he paused for a moment to draw a breath.

Then he threw the door open and charged into the abandoned storeroom that was his secret chamber, sword raised and ready to strike.

He stopped in the middle of the floor. There was no one here. But the place had changed. Poised like a heroic statue, sword still on high, he kept turning about, amazed at what he saw.

The room had been straightened up. Dust and debris were gone, and all his booty—all the fine articles of gold and silver, all the fine jewelry—was arranged in neat piles on shelves and on and about the floor. Treasure chests, jewelry boxes and other containers were arrayed in rows. Instead of a jumble of expensive junk there was now an orderly selection, as in a dealer's stall at some bazaar.

Slowly, he lowered his sword.

"What in the name of—?"

He took a quick inventory, moving about the room and sorting through everything. He opened strongboxes, used his sword to stir up the metallic stew of gold and silver coins. He counted necklaces and trinkets, gold plates and chalices, everything.

Done, he could not ascertain that there was one item missing. But he was not satisfied. He counted and sorted and itemized again.

Finally he gave up. No, nothing had been filched, not a bauble missing. All his swag was present and accounted for.

He sheathed his sword, closed a trunk, and sat. He pondered long and hard. Servants? No, this was too far from the living quarters of the keep. Servants never came here. Nor did anybody, for this was one of the wilder areas of the castle.

Who, then? Why did they tidy up? Why did they not take anything?

He decided to put it down to castle strangeness. Yes. The storeroom was located in one of the more unstable areas of the fortress, and that meant that anything could happen. The floor could disappear beneath your feet. Walls could shift and slide. And baffling, anomalous things could happen, including a room deciding to tidy itself up.

Yes, that must be it. Castle strangeness. Put it down to that and forget it. Well, he must give some thought to relocating his stash. That would be a bother, yes. But think on it he must. To say the least. In fact, moving would be the prudent thing to do in any case. But why in the name of all the gods . . . ?

Yes, the vagaries of living in Castle Perilous. The uncertainties, the risks. He looked about him. Aye, and the rewards.

When he'd first blundered into Perilous he was shocked by the alien strangeness of the place. The stuff of legend and myth. After recovering from this initial disorientation, he began to cast his thieving eyes about for professional opportunities, for all castles worth their salt had treasure rooms. Knowing this, he looked high and low.

And had come up empty-handed. If the castle had a treasure house it had eluded Kwip completely. And well it might, for the castle was enchanted beyond his powers of comprehension, and any valuables therein would doubtless be under magical protection.

So, he had widened his search for loot into the sundry magical worlds of the castle's aspects. All this booty had come from forays into other realms, into myriad fairy kingdoms and countless enchanted lands. He had traveled far and wide and come back laden each trip. And he'd dumped the stuff here.

To what purpose, though? What would he do with it all?

He'd often asked himself that. Perhaps he simply needed something to do. Perhaps . . . just to keep his hand in his trade?

No matter. Whatever the reason, stealing was his profession, the only one he knew.

Something nettled him. This damned business. He flatly didn't believe the castle theory. Someone had been in here, someone now knew of his doings. He had to find out who that person was.

But first, he had to move all the swag. A major effort. He picked up an inlaid box of trinkets and tucked it under his arm, then thought better of it and set it back down. No, would find a new place first, then come back and begin making trips.

But what if the intruder returned? Unsettling possibility. Perhaps he went to fetch help, confederates. There was too much loot for one man. Yes, that was it. The thieves would be back in force. Well, he'd simply wait for them.

But . . . what if there were too many of them?

He picked up the inlaid box again. First, get the stuff out of here, as fast as possible. Shove it all in his room in the Guest wing. Under the bed, in the wardrobe, closets, whatever. Fast. *Now.* Then . . . well, then he'd think what to do next. The important thing was speed.

He put the box down yet again and began filling his pockets with the loose stuff.

Club Sheila

THE PARTY HAD WOUND DOWN. The bartenders were washing glasses, the caterers busy cleaning scraps off the food tables. The moon hung low in the sky, hiding under drooping palms, as the night grew ever older. The big Victorian-style hotel was dark and quiet, the sound of the breaking surf muffled by a rising night breeze.

A group of castle Guests were still at it, though, sitting in lawn chairs by the pool, quietly drinking—among them Deena Williams, a black woman from Brooklyn. She was dressed in a bright orange chemise and had her hair done in an acorn cut.

Barnaby Walsh occupied the chaise next to her. Plump and pale of face, he sat raptly listening to Melanie McDaniel's guitar variations on an Irish folk melody.

Everyone else was talking.

"I'm through drinkin'," Deena said, setting her Mai Tai down on the umbrella table next to her. "I'm over my limit now."

"You don't seem intoxicated," the man everyone called M. DuQuesne told her. He was in evening dress: black tie, boiled shirt, patent leather pumps. Which wasn't unusual for him; in fact, he always dressed formally. He spoke English fluently but with a heavy accent. "What is your limit, by the way?"

"Six."

"Six Mai Tais?"

"Six of anything. Six beers, even."

"Well, it's been a nice affair. I quite enjoyed myself."

"I didn't say I didn't enjoy myself. If I have another Mai Tai, I'm gonna have to be towed back to the castle."

"No, I was just commenting, dear." M. DuQuesne looked around. "Seems everyone has left. Almost everyone, anyway."

"I wonder what time it is, castle time. I don't feel sleepy."

DuQuesne looked at his watch. "Good reason. It's rather late in the afternoon at the castle."

"Is that all? Hell, I might as well have another drink. Waiter!"

"You haven't finished that one," DuQuesne said, pointing.

Deena looked. "Oh." She picked up the glass and drank.

A man with a German accent sitting next to DuQuesne said, "Perhaps you should switch to something less sweet, Deena. That is a very fancy concoction to be drinking so many of."

"I like 'em. Can't be too sweet for me. I got a sweet tooth."

Thaxton and Dalton came walking across the tennis courts. Thaxton had to be steered a bit.

"Hey," Deena called. "How'd your moonlight swim go?"

"Excellent," Dalton said. "His lordship passed out on the beach."

"Didn't so much pass out, old boy, as took a bit of a nap."

"Right."

Deena asked, "Where're your lady friends?"

"Don't quite know," Dalton said. "They seem to have left us."

"Swam away, they did," Thaxton contended as he slumped to a deck chair. "Mermaids. Lovely sea horses. Sea mares. Farewell, farewell."

"Boy, he's flyin'," Deena said.

"He's cruising at about thirty-five thousand feet," Dalton confirmed.

"Perfectly sober, old boy. Perfectly sober."

"Perfectly smashed," Deena countered.

"Nonsense. By the way, can a fellow get a drink in this place?" Thaxton turned and called, "*Garçon!*"

Deena asked, "Who's this Garson guy people been callin' all night?"

"No, my dear, that's French for—"

Deena shot daggers at DuQuesne. "It's a *joke*, stupid. don't you think I know that?"

M. DuQuesne was somewhat flustered. "Very sorry, my dear."

"Forget it." Deena leaned back wearily. "Uh-oh."

"What, Deena?"

"I'm turnin' into a mean drunk. When that happens, I *gotta* stop drinkin'." Deena set her glass aside.

"Don't worry about it," M. DuQuesne said.

"No, no matter what time it is, I gotta get me some sleep. Hey, who's heading back to the castle?"

Melanie stopped playing. "Me. Party's just about over, looks like." She reached for her guitar case.

"I will say good night," the German-speaking gentleman

said. He got up and walked off. "Very glad to see you all. Nice party."

"Goo' night, Karl baby," Deena said. "Nice talkin' with ya, honey."

"Good night."

"Here comes old Gene," Dalton observed.

Hands in his pockets, Gene came walking through the courts to join the group.

"Yo," he said.

"Gene, where you been?" Deena asked. "Takin' a moonlight swim with some new hot momma?"

"Sure." Gene sat in one of the deck chairs.

"Where's Linda?"

"Don't know."

"Where'd she get to, anyhow? I ain't seen her in a while."

"We saw her last with Gene on the beach," Dalton tattled.

"What? Gene, was you out there skinny dippin' with Linda?"

Gene shook his head. "Nope. She went back to the castle a while ago."

"You was, you gonna have to answer to me."

"No such luck."

"They were wrestling in the sand," Dalton said. "I think that's what they were doing."

"What the hell you talkin' about? Him and *Linda*? You crazy."

"All in fun," Gene said.

"Must be, 'cause Linda don't fool around with nobody."

"Nope." Gene sighed.

"She got principles."

"Yup."

"She don't go sleepin' around."

Gene's chin sank to his chest. "Negative."

"How come you never asked me?"

Gene jerked his head up. "Huh?"

"You go takin' after Linda. You go takin' after everybody, this universe, that universe, boppin' 'em over, one, two, three, draggin' 'em back by the hair. And here I have to sleep alone. Shit." Deena reached and had another go at her Mai Tai.

"Had I known—" Gene began.

"Had you known shit, fool." Deena gave her head a quick shake. "Man, I must be flyin' myself."

Melanie had to suppress a giggle.

"Well, I'm going to head back to the castle," Barnaby Walsh announced.

"Don't *you* talk to me, either."

"Who's talking to you?"

Deena told everyone, "Last time he left his shoes under my bed he was wearin' baby sneakers."

"Deena, you're smashed."

"Don't I know it. I'm gonna regret it in the mornin'."

"I'm regretting it now," Barnaby said, getting up.

"Where's that bloody waiter?" Thaxton demanded to know.

"Is Lord Peter a mean drunk, too?" Deena asked suspiciously.

"I've never seen him drunk before," Dalton said. "A bit tipsy, perhaps."

"I'm not drunk!" Thaxton insisted. "Where is that—? Oh, well, finally."

A white-jacketed waiter came over. "Yes, sir?"

"I'd like a bottle of your finest plonk—Chateau Fleet Street will do nicely."

"Sir, I'm afraid you've had enough for the evening."

Thaxton bristled. "I *beg* your pardon?"

"Sorry, sir. You're intoxicated and I can't serve you. Hotel policy. Insurance regulations, sir."

"Excuse me. What is your name?"

"Fenton, sir."

"Tell me this, Fenton. Are you a real flesh-and-blood human being, or are you simply part of the window dressing here?"

"Sir?"

"You know very well what I'm talking about. Are you real or are you not?"

"Well, I suppose . . . not quite, sir."

"Ah. Not quite. And you—a bloody phantasm conjured out of the ether by some bloody mumbo jumbo—are presuming to tell me when and how much I can drink?"

"Sir, I am. Lady Sheila's orders, sir."

The wind spilled out of Thaxton's sails. "Blast. Oh, bugger all, get me a cup of coffee, then."

"Right away, sir." Fenton spun on his heel and left.

Dalton regarded Thaxton archly. "Do you want me to send for the pukka boy now so you can whip him?"

"Well, he was impertinent!"

"These aren't the great days of the Raj, Thaxton, old boy."

"Never bloody said they were."

Deena cranked her tired body upward. "Come on, everybody . . . *uhhh* . . . let's head back." She got to her feet, teetering.

Rising, M. DuQuesne said, "Good idea."

"Let's go, Colonel-sahib," Dalton said with a squeeze to Thaxton's shoulder.

"But my coffee—?"

"We'll drop into the dining hall for a late snack," Dalton said, looking at his watch, "or actually tea, to be more precise. It's about five P.M. castle time."

"I could eat again," Deena said. "Count me in."

Thaxton in tow, they all trooped into the hotel, making a ragged beeline for the elevators.

"Well, I wasn't being nasty at all, so far as I can see," Thaxton was arguing as they all emerged from the lift and stepped into the stone stronghold of the castle keep. "Just asserting my rights."

"You were downright beastly," Dalton scolded, "and I'm calling you on it."

"See here, that's hardly a fair characterization of the incident," Thaxton said, the hint of a petulant whine to his voice.

"Let's drop it."

"I'm more than willing."

"This group better stay away from alcohol," Deena said as they walked along the corridor. "You guys and booze don't mix."

"Demon rum," Gene mused.

"Yeah, that ol' demon'll getcha every time."

They passed through an intersecting corridor. No one saw the odd gnomish creature as it crossed behind them, broom in hand.

"Actually, I rarely drink," Gene said. "Just on social occasions."

"I like bein' social."

"A social drinker. Actually, I'm a socialist drinker."

Deena shot him a curious look. "What the hell's a socialist drinker?"

"One who believes in the collective ownership of the means of distillation."

"Damn, there he goes again. Talkin' crazy."

Dalton said, "Quite a novel political concept you have there, Gene."

"Yeah, but I don't advocate the violent overthrow of the existing distillation system. That's what separates a gradualist like me from—"

Gene stopped in his tracks at the sight of the approaching apparition: a broom-bearing gnome in bib overalls. Everyone halted with him.

They all stood watching as the creature passed. It moved with a curious bobbing gait, head swaying, its misshapen eyes averted.

When it turned a corner and was gone, Deena said, "What the *hell* was that?"

Dalton rubbed his sharp chin. "You know, I've seen all manner of strange critters in this place. But there's something about that one, something odd."

"Yeah," Barnaby Walsh said. "What do you think it was?"

"A homunculus," Gene replied. "Horrible little malformed thing. Reminds me of a film producer I once knew."

"Dwarf, gnome," Dalton offered.

"Hobbit?" Gene ventured. "No, its feet weren't hairy."

"No, you're right. 'Homunculus' is *le mot juste*."

"What's the problem?" Thaxton wanted to know. "As you said yourself, Dalton, old boy, not a day goes by when we don't see some abomination in the castle. Frightful beasties at every turn."

"But that thing is *passing* strange," Dalton insisted.

"Wouldn't have given it a second thought if you hadn't—"

Yet another homunculus, pink and bald and dressed in blue bib overalls, turned the corner ahead and came toward them.

Dalton said, "You were saying?"

"Bloody hell."

As before, the creature shambled by without giving them so much as a passing glance.

"Weird shit goin' on here," Deena muttered. "I'm goin' to bed. Good night, y'all." She hurried down the corridor.

"Wait, we'll walk you," Gene called after her.

"My room's right down the hall," Deena told him as she paused at the next intersection to peer around the corner. She checked both directions before heading left.

The rest of the group turned right toward the Queen's Dining Hall.

"Well, it's probably nothing," Thaxton said. "A few stray creatures fallen in from one balmy universe or another. God knows there are enough of them in this place. Balmy universes, that is."

"Nothing to it, huh?" Dalton asked as yet another homunculus crossed their path.

Thaxton stopped and put his fists to his hips. "Something is going on."

"Why brooms, do you think?" Gene wondered.

"Brooms," Dalton pondered. "Haven't a clue."

"Could they be a new type of servant?" Melanie asked.

"Now there's a rational explanation," Dalton said. "Maybe the Chamberlain knows something."

"Let's go up to Edwin's quarters and ask him," Gene suggested.

"We should ask Tyrene," Thaxton said. "If the Captain of the Guard doesn't know about this, he should be informed."

Dalton began, "I do believe—" but was interrupted by a shout.

"What's the matter?" Gene called to Deena as she came running up the corridor.

"They're in my room!" she cried out. "Little guys!"

"In your—?"

They all rushed to Deena's quarters.

The door was wide open.

"They're in there . . . *cleanin'*!" Deena wailed. "They're sweepin' up my goddamn room!"

"Maybe they're supposed to?" Dalton said, half-suggesting, half-disbelieving.

"I sure as hell don't want 'em to! Ain't I got any say in it?"

They all peeked around the doorjamb. Sure enough, inside were four of the curious creatures, furiously but efficiently tidying up the bedroom, brooms whisking, rags snapping. The faint scent of lemon oil arose from the place.

"Damnedest thing," Thaxton said.

MYKOS

THE GATE TO THE CITY was an imposing structure topped by two stone lions confronting each other. The gate itself consisted of immense bronze doors that opened onto the main avenue of the citadel. The walls of Mykos were made of great blocks of stone, fitted one to another with extreme precision. From afar the buildings and temples of the city looked modern. No columns crowned with acanthus, no friezes. No statuary save for the lions. This was not a classical age. The city within the gates was the stronghold of a warlord.

The gatekeeper was a spear-carrying soldier wearing a helmet made of segments of ivory—probably boar's tusks—sewn together and stitched to a leather lining. He wore bronze greaves and a leather breastplate over his red tunic.

"Halt and state your name and your business."

"I am Trent, brother of Inkarnases the magician. Here is his signet to prove it. I am here at the behest of His Majesty the king."

The guard took one look at the ring.

"You are expected, Honorable. Please enter. If it please you, an escort will be provided to the royal palace."

"It pleases me. I thank you kindly."

Trent was waved through the gate. Inside, he was met by two more spear-carriers who bade him follow them. This he did, and found himself touring the citadel by foot.

He was still amazed at how clean and functional the architecture looked. He had half-expected porticos and Corinthian façades. But this was not Greece, nor was it an analogue to the Greece of Pericles. If this world corresponded with any earthly period, it evoked a dim past that was mostly legend. However prehistoric, though, the architecture was not primitive by any means. It was functional and graceful at the same time. Its lines were sharply geometrical, unadorned, yet comfortably human, quite unlike the rigid, uncompromising Bauhaus style of another universe and another time.

This curious style diverged from the modern in another way: the buildings were painted in very bright, sometimes gaudy colors.

A gradually rising earthen ramp gave him a sweeping view. On the city's western fringe lay a circular wall that enclosed what looked like a cemetery with huge stones marking grave sites. To the east stood an enclave of simple buildings that probably housed artisans and their workshops. Beyond them lay a section of more elaborate structures that might have been the digs of royal functionaries or perhaps the clergy.

The ramp led up to the foot of a broad stone stairway, which mounted to the summit of the eminence that commanded the plains below, and to the acropolis, whereon stood the palace and the various temples.

Trent lagged behind his escort, and they slowed their pace to accommodate him. Ancient history had never held any special attraction for him, but this milieu was greatly interesting.

One of the soldiers glanced back at him curiously, and he increased his pace. He'd be here a while; time enough later to rubberneck.

The entrance to the palace complex was a narrow gate set in a high wall enclosing a courtyard.

The palace itself was imposing, painted in bright colors that looked at once barbaric and decadent. The massive tapered columns flanking the entrance were iridescent red, banded in yellow and blue.

He followed his escort through the columns and into a spacious entry hall, where he was announced to the palace guards. These detached two of their number to lead him through high corridors and into the palace proper.

They passed through a smaller courtyard, then threaded two more huge pillars, entering another corridor, at the end of which was a vestibule that gave access to a great hall. This high chamber was done in a color scheme even more garish than that of the exterior.

Bright shades of all the primary hues were represented in stripes, bands, and zigzags. Cryptic signs and patterns abounded, among them stars, crosses, and, disconcertingly, swastikas (an ancient symbol in many worlds, it would seem). Bordered by the decorations, frescoes depicting animals and birds festooned the walls.

The roof was supported by four huge columns, decorated like those of the façade, surrounding a circular fire pit. Cut into the ceiling directly above the pit was a skylight, a canopy with open sides, intended to ward off rain, let in light, and, presumably, let out smoke. But not at the moment. The fire pit was cold and the hall was dark.

After asking Trent to wait, one of the guards continued through the room and went out a doorway at the back.

A curiously stylized seat, looking rather uncomfortable, stood against the right wall. A throne? If so, this hall was the court of Anthaemion.

The other guard smiled but said nothing. Trent smiled back, then walked a few steps to look up through the skylight. The sky was coldly blue. This was a sunny clime, but the temperature was a bit chilly today. He wrapped his cloak more closely about him.

He wondered if Incarnadine's language-infusion spell would work as well as advertised. Inky had touted it, assuring Trent that he would have no trouble understanding the local tongue or making himself understood. The exchange with the guards had been minimal, so it was still hard to gauge how much of a problem communicating would be. The audience with Anthaemion would be the test. The conversation would necessitate some subtlety, always difficult to achieve in a foreign tongue, magic or none. Nuance was the stock in trade of diplomats. He would have liked to have some idea as to how much nuance he was capable of conveying. Or would it be better to go for a more direct approach? Maybe trickery was the key. Take advantage of the language barrier and obfuscate like hell.

The unsettling thing about infused-knowledge techniques was that you sometimes didn't know what you knew.

A man in a red and yellow tunic came through the back entrance. Dark-haired and tall, he walked slowly and with aplomb. As he approached he smiled warmly.

"Greetings, Trent, brother of Inkarnases. You honor this house by your visit."

"I am honored in turn by this great house."

"His Majesty presents his compliments, and asks that you be received in his chambers. He is taking his midday meal."

"Gladly will I be received."

"I am Telamon, chamberlain to His Majesty."

Trent bowed.

Telamon seemed pleased with this gesture, though Trent was not sure it was appropriate.

"If you will walk with me . . . ?"

They left the throne room and went through a wide corridor, at the end of which was a staircase. This they mounted to a second story.

"Your brother does not speak much of the land you hail from," Telamon said. "I have always been curious as to what it is like there."

"It is bleak and drear, I'm afraid."

"So? Like our land, somewhat. Nothing but rocks, mountains, thin soil—aside from the plains below, from which we eke a living. This is a poor land, really."

"Yet Mykos seems affluent."

"Yes, we are supposed to be rich in gold. And we have gold, but little more than any other city of importance. We make a great show of it to impress the farmers and shepherds. But our reputation for riches and high living is for the most part undeserved. We are a simple people."

"Nevertheless I am very impressed with your city."

This also pleased Telamon. "We like it. The gods have favored us. We owe it all to them."

So far, so good, Trent thought.

Telamon asked, "Are you aware that Menoetius visits us?"

Trent thumbed through the file of names in the part of his mind that had been magically stuffed with data.

"Brother to His Majesty, and King of Lakonis. No, I was not aware. I look forward to our meeting."

"He does know Inkarnases, but not well. You are aware that it was Menoetius' request for aid that precipitated this crisis?"

"Uh, yes. It was his wife, Queen Alena, who was abducted."

"By Pelion, son of Proetus, King of Dardania. It is the scandal of all Arkadia." Telamon halted Trent with a gentle touch. He whispered, "And Menoetius' shame. The gossips have it that she went willingly after falling in love with Pelion the moment she set eyes on him. I needn't warn you to refrain from characterizing it as anything but a kidnapping in Menoetius' presence?"

"You needn't. Inkarnases has briefed me."

"I had assumed, but wanted to sound you out on the matter before your audience."

"I understand," Trent said. "Perhaps you should test me further on my knowledge of things in general. I understand that the abduction precipitated the crisis. Menoetius appealed to Anthaemion, and the latter used his influence to forge the coalition against Dardania. This must be elementary to you, but all the information I have is raw and undigested. I am a complete stranger to your land."

"I quite understand," Telamon said. "But your brother spoke so highly of your skills that I have every confidence that the finer points will become second nature to you before long. Besides, the situation at Piraeon—"

"Pardon, where?"

"Where the coalition fleet is anchored. As I say, the situation there is not good. Much disagreement."

"So I have heard."

"And so fortunately for you, and unfortunately for the strategic situation, we have more time than we want."

They had come to a door flanked by two sets of three guards each, spears at their sides, except for the two nearest the door, who had theirs crossed. At the sight of the two men coming down the hall, they pulled back their weapons to permit entry.

Telamon led Trent into a narrow vestibule and thence into the apartment beyond. It was a smaller version of the megaron, the great hall downstairs, but here the fire pit was blazing, and off to one side were two men in fine robes lounging on low recliners, eating an elaborate meal. The food was being served on gold dishes by a trio of female servants with dark braided hair, dressed in long layered gowns. All three were pretty. From decorated amphorae they poured thick syrupy wine into gold cups.

The older of the two men was gray-bearded and corpulent, with deep-set dark eyes and a prominent nose. The younger man resembled him, but he was thinner, and his eyes were smaller and somehow less intelligent, though he had an intense look about him.

Telamon stopped some distance away. Trent waited behind him. The men talked and ate. Presently the gray-bearded man looked up and nodded to Telamon. Telamon approached.

"Majesty, may I present Trent, brother of Inkarnases."

Trent stepped forward and bowed deeply.

The gray-bearded one—presumably Anthaemion, King of Mykos—frowned. "Trent," he said as he picked his teeth with a fingernail. "Trent. Odd name."

"May it please His Majesty."

"It pleases me not that your brother has chosen to absent himself from my court during this crisis."

Uh-oh, Trent thought. Had Inky underestimated or dissembled?

"Uh, pressing business, Your Majesty. He said—"

"I know what he said. He is a most persuasive man. He said you would be the better military adviser. Is he right?"

"I will serve His Majesty to the utmost limit of my talents."

"If you're half as clever as your brother, you'll do fine. You've been informed of the details of our situation?"

"Yes, sire."

"Forces available, enemy tactics, that sort of thing?"

"As much as Inkarnases knows, I know."

"What he knows is considerable," the king said. "How he knows so much is a mystery to me, but I don't presume to understand the ways of sorcerers. We did not even possess an accurate map of the Dardanian coast until he divined one. I presume you are a magician also?"

"I am, sire."

"How good a one? Can you win this war for me by simply casting a spell?"

"That would be a difficult way of going about it, sire. No one enchantment could take into account all the myriad contingencies."

"That's what your brother said. I believe him. But you can cast spells to provide favorable conditions, facilitate the happy unfolding of events, forfend hexes and other dangers—all that?"

"All that can be done, sire."

The king nodded. "Good. We'll need every supernatural advantage. In addition to the favor of the gods."

The king's brother spoke: "Surely the gods favor those who are wronged, as I have been."

"No doubt," the king told him.

The smell of herbs and spices came to Trent's nostrils: fennel, coriander, and others he couldn't identify. He hoped the food here wasn't too spicy. The stuff looked good, anyway. Both men continued eating as they talked.

The king went on. "But it's not that simple, I'm afraid. There are gods, and there are gods. They divide and take opposite sides. Some no doubt favor our enemy. I myself have had disturbing dreams of late."

Menoetius raised his eyebrows. "Oh? What dreams are these?"

Anthaemion shook his head. "I cannot recount them clearly enough to make sense. I half-remember them. Perhaps, as time goes on, their import will be made clearer. But they are disturbing nonetheless."

"This does not bode well."

Anthaemion's brow lowered. "No. Some days I sit and brood, and it occurs to me that what we aim to do will not go well, that no good can come of it."

"But our honor must be restored."

The king half-smiled. "Our honor, brother?"

"Pelion's outrage was an affront to all Arkadians!"

Anthaemion popped a honeyed fig into his mouth, chewed thoughtfully, then swallowed before answering. "Of course, my brother. Of course. But there are other reasons why we must deal with the Dardanians. The price of grain rises every year, and we must import more every year. We need new fields to till, and there are none to have in this barren wilderness. The Dardanian coast has vast fertile plains lying fallow, waiting for the bite of the plow, but the Dardanians burn our colonies and kill our colonists, or take them prisoner. Niggardly of them, is it not? No, favorite brother, there are other good reasons for our attempting to rescue Alena from the clutches of the rapist Pelion."

"Foul rapist and pirate. Whom I will first castrate, then rip his belly open for dogs to devour the guts, while I watch and enjoy. That is but a taste of what I will do to Pelion when I take Troas."

The king chuckled. "You will reduce Troas alone, then?"

Menoetius looked into his gold wine cup. "Not alone, no. But I will challenge Pelion to come out and face me. Alone."

"Single combat settles nothing," Anthaemion said.

"I demand the right."

Anthaemion sighed. "As I suppose you must. Brave of you, my brother. Very brave."

The king looked up at Trent again. "As you can see, there are many complications to this affair. I have not begun to mention them. Half our forces are at the other half's throat. Ancient enmities, old vendettas. It is the way of our people. Nevertheless, we are united in one single purpose, to destroy the Dardanians once and for all. And that we will, the gods willing. I would meet with you again, Trent. Tomorrow morning. My brother goes back to Piraeon then. Tomorrow you will tell me your ideas of how best to attack the Dardanian coast and where to deploy our armies to greatest advantage."

Trent bowed. "Sire, I will be happy to do so."

Right. Trent thought, *all my brilliant ideas, of which I've come up with zero to date.*

"Meanwhile, dine and sleep. Take what slave girls you want to your bed. They seem to breed of late. More mouths to feed. Gods know how I got so many of them. You may go."

Telamon and Trent bowed, then backed away.

"I'll show you to your quarters," Telamon told him in the vestibule. "Very comfortable, with a view of the plains."

Trent thought, *Inky, I'm going to kill you one of these days. Just a matter of time.*

QUEEN'S DINING HALL

"I SAY WE SPLIT UP into pairs and fan out," Dalton said as he stirred his coffee.

"Not a bad idea," Gene said. "We only have to check 144,000 holes to see which one they might be coming through."

"True, it's a huge job."

"Though I suppose it's got to be done."

"Right."

"Because, even as we speak . . ."

Three homunculi were busy sweeping up the dining room. As Gene and his friends watched, two more came in to help.

"But he can't check every aspect," Thaxton said.

"Let's hope we get lucky," Dalton said.

"And what exactly is our plan when we do find the portal the little beggars are coming through?"

Dalton shrugged and sipped his coffee.

"I'll tell you what we do," Deena Williams said. "We get some bricks and mortar and wall up that damn hole."

"A thought," Thaxton said.

"It's spooky." Deena shivered.

"No, we let Lord Incarnadine deal with them," Barnaby Walsh said.

"How come he ain't dealin' with 'em now?"

"Well, I don't know. I suppose—"

"Hey, *there* she is," Deena said.

Everyone looked up at Linda as she came walking over to the long dining table.

"Hi, gang."

"Linda, where you been?"

"Following little strange critters."

"So have we," Dalton said. "Did you happen to find out where they're coming from?"

"Nope," Linda said, pouring herself some coffee. "Tried. They're all over the place."

"Craziest thing," Deena said, shaking her head. "They give me the creeps."

"Oh, they're cute, in a way," Linda said, watching one of them diligently sweep by.

"Cute? They're disgustin', that's what they are."

"Aw, not really. They remind me of Elmer Fudd."

"I don't care if they look like Bugs Bunny. I want 'em outta here."

"How many of them are there, do you think?" Thaxton asked of the group.

"I counted hundreds," Linda said. "Hundreds and hundreds. No matter where I went, there they were."

"There are very possibly thousands of them," Dalton said. "Even so, I don't think the castle's in any immediate danger. In any event, we really should inform Tyrene."

"I saw him," Linda said. "Upstairs in the gymnasium, chasing the little devils around. He and some of the Guards. Until they gave up. There were over three hundred of them just in there."

"They seem to be increasing geometrically," Dalton said.

"And they don't say a word," Thaxton said. "Not a bloody word."

"We'll see," Gene said, getting to his feet. One of the homunculi was sweeping a path toward him. He got in front of it.

"Excuse me. Uh, say, little buddy . . ."

It began to sweep a circle around him.

"Yo! Hey, there. Have a minute?" Gene shifted position to block the diminutive creature's path.

It turned and began to sweep in the opposite direction.

Gene reached and grabbed the creature by the shoulder straps where they crossed at the back. The little fellow immediately went limp.

Gene picked the thing up.

"Doesn't weigh much at all."

"Gene, be careful!" Linda said. "You might hurt it."

"Not to worry."

Gene gently lowered the creature to the floor and let go of the straps. After a moment, its head came up. Then it moved away from Gene, beginning its task once again, applying the broom quickly, methodically, sedulously.

"Completely passive," Dalton said. "Can't see how they'd be any danger at all. Just a nuisance."

"But what if they don't stop comin' through?" Deena demanded.

"The castle's a big place," Dalton said. "We have some time yet before we're hip-deep in them."

"Surely Incarnadine can deal with them," Thaxton said. Dalton asked Linda, "Have you seen him lately?"

"I asked Tyrene if he'd told the king. He said he has men out trying to locate him."

"He probably knows already," Thaxton said. "And is already dealing with the matter."

"Maybe the king suddenly took off on one of his extended sojourns," Gene suggested.

"He was at the party when I left," Linda said.

"I saw him leave with Trent," Barnaby Walsh said.

"That's right, he did," Dalton agreed.

"I shouldn't think they went far," Thaxton said.

"Hope not," Linda said.

"But what if Incarnadine can't deal with these little guys?" Deena asked nervously.

Heads turned as two more little guys with brooms entered the room.

"Then I suppose we'll have to learn to live with them," Dalton commented.

"Not me!" Deena said. "That happens, I'm pickin' an aspect an' puttin' my bod right through it. I ain't never comin' back."

"We're hardly at that point yet," Thaxton said. "Don't fret."

"Too late, I'm frettin' already."

Gene said, "I say we take Cleve's suggestion. Split up and reconnoiter, report back here in, say, two hours."

"We'll never find out where they're coming from," Deena said.

"If we find areas of the castle where they aren't, that will whittle down the possibilities a bit. I can't believe they're all over the castle yet. They're coming from somewhere, and we should find out where that somewhere is."

"What if the source isn't an aspect?" Dalton asked.

Gene shrugged. "What are the other possibilities?"

"Yes, where else could they be coming from?" Thaxton asked.

Dalton thought about it for a moment. Then he said, "The castle itself."

Gene nodded. "I guess it's possible."

"Another version of castle instability," Dalton went on. "We've run into all kinds. Walls shaking, parts of the place disappearing. Remember the apparitions? Well, this may be another variety of them."

"These critters seem a little too real," Linda said.

"True," Dalton conceded.

"Which is why we have to eliminate the possibility of another invasion," Gene said. "These guys could be the setup for a takeover."

Thaxton laughed. "By tidying up? The invaders are sticklers for cleanliness, are they?"

"Stranger things have happened in this castle," Dalton said.

"Well, I'll admit anything's possible. But surely an invasion's out. I mean, I've heard of mopping up, but—"

"We'd better get started," Gene urged. "The wider the dispersion gets, the harder it'll be to pinpoint the center of it."

"Gene's right," Dalton said.

"Thing is," Linda put in, "everywhere I went in the keep, there they were."

"How far did you get?" Gene asked.

"Pretty far into the west wing. Down about ten floors. Gene, they're probably all over the keep."

Gene shook his head glumly. "Then we'll never find the hole they're pouring through."

Dalton said, "But we really should give it a try, shouldn't we?"

"Better to have a go at finding Incarnadine, maybe?" Thaxton suggested.

Deena agreed. "Now there's an idea. And Trent, too. We're gonna need all the help we can get."

"And Sheila," Linda said. "Speaking of super magicians. We might have to improvise until the king gets back, if he went anywhere."

Dalton started to say, "Nevertheless, some of us—"

Everybody cocked an ear.

"What is it?" Deena asked.

They all listened.

Deena seemed annoyed. "Music?"

The sound of a far-off drum grew closer. Accompanying it, a flute or pipe. The rhythm was exotic and infectious.

"I hear music," Dalton confirmed.

"*Now* what the hell is goin' on?" Deena despaired.

"Whatever it is," Gene said, "it's coming this way. Pass the sugar, will you, Lord Peter?"

Thaxton handed him the pewter sugar bowl.

"Thank you."

In a few moments the source was revealed. A belly dancer—an extremely shapely one—came shivering and shaking into the dining hall. Accompanying her were two musicians, a drummer and a piper, in vaguely Arabic dress.

They proceeded to put on a show. Everybody watched.

The woman whirled and clanged her finger cymbals, slinking up to the men and undulating suggestively. She danced twice around the table and then began to writhe and twirl out of the room, followed by the musicians.

Linda watched with interest. "She's really good," was her comment to Gene.

"Uh, yeah."

"Beautiful woman!" Dalton enthused.

"Uh, yeah," Gene said.

"Very charming," Thaxton observed.

"However do they do that—?" Dalton made motions in front of his stomach.

"Diaphragm exercises," Thaxton said.

Before the first dancer-musician troupe got to the door, another entered and began to repeat the whole routine, threading their way through the ever-growing clot of broom-wielding homunculi. The group at the table sat and watched this performance as well, though a little less appreciatively.

"Charming, absolutely charming," Thaxton remarked. "But you know, I'm beginning to get worried."

"Housecleaning homunculi," Dalton pondered, drumming the table with his long fingers. "And belly dancers." He thought about it a while." Then he gave sigh. "Frankly, I don't see the connection.

Gene said, "Well, it's all so obvious, isn't it?"

Gene calmly drank his coffee as yet another distant drum drew nearer.

Deena said, "Uh-oh."

GAMING HALL

JEREMY HOCHSTEADER WAS DRESSED in a parti-colored cote-
hardie (a longish tunic belted at the waist) in black and
orange with matching tights: one leg per color. His orange
Reebok cross-training shoes somehow looked appropriate.

He was sitting at a table playing a home video game and
enjoying it. He had been invited to the party at Club Sheila
of course, but he didn't like parties, so he'd put off going
until it was too late.

No less than three homunculi had swept out the room
already, but Jeremy hadn't paid them any mind, his attention fixed on wheels of fire and vicious turtles. But now he
heard music; and though he didn't stop playing, he was
beginning to grow aware that something might be going on.
Maybe Sheila's party had spilled over into the castle.

Maybe it had. So what.

He kept playing, thumbing the buttons on the control
device, jumping over pitfalls and leapfrogging monsters.
The music grew louder but he still didn't care. He wished
whoever was making it would go away.

The commotion entered the gaming hall but he still didn't

turn around. There came quite a racket and Jeremy was beginning to get annoyed.

He stopped the game's action and looked toward the entrance.

"What the heck is this?"

Belly dancers? There were three of them, and with them a bunch of little guys playing weird instruments. The beauty of the women stunned him a bit before he began wondering if the castle was going nuts again. It did that periodically.

They danced around the hall and then circled him, clanging things in his face. He kind of liked looking at the women, but he thought the music sucked.

Presently the whole kit and caboodle bumped and ground their way out of the hall. The high-pitched flutes were the last to fade. But in their wake came the sounds of some other disturbance.

"Screwy," Jeremy said.

But that was life in the castle. You never knew what was going to come jumping out of the woodwork . . . or the masonry, or whatever.

Melanie McDaniel came walking in carrying her lute. She was dressed in a troubadour's outfit: black velvet cap with a feather, black velvet doublet, silver-gray cloak, scarlet tights, and black shoes. It was her usual mode of dress for going about the castle; she had stopped into her room to change after the party.

"Have you been seeing the weird stuff?" she asked.

"Just saw it," Jeremy said.

"There's more, all over."

"Yeah? What's going on?"

"Nobody seems to know."

"Any trouble?"

"Well, no, not trouble, really. It's just very bizarre."

"So what else is new?"

Jeremy turned back to his video game.

Melanie asked, "Have you seen the little guys sweeping up?"

"Huh? What little guys?"

"Little buggers this tall"—she held her hand two or three feet above the floor—"in blue bib overalls. With brooms. They sweep up all over the place."

Jeremy's memory was jogged. "Oh. Yeah, I saw them. What are they all about?"

"Nobody knows that either."

"Weird."

"Uh-oh."

Jeremy turned his head. "What?"

More belly dancers entered. This time there were a good half dozen or more.

Disgusted, Jeremy threw down the control box and turned off the monitor. He swiveled around on the high stool, crossed his legs, and watched.

Melanie sat on the edge of the table and watched with him.

At length she commented, "These women really can dance."

"Say what?"

"I said . . . Never mind."

This troupe didn't want to leave—or did it only seem that way because more dancers were coming in to take the place of the ones who left? It was hard to tell.

Finally Jeremy got up and said, "Let's get the heck out of here."

Melanie picked up her lute. "I'm with you."

They weaved their way to the archway and ducked out.

The corridor was less crowded, but only by comparison. Gnomish sweepers swept by, and Jeremy wondered why he hadn't really noticed them before. They sure were weird-looking. Vaguely familiar, too. Porky Pig? No, maybe . . .

"Oh, look."

Jeremy looked left. A chorus line of colorfully costumed and gorgeous women was high-kicking its way down the corridor. All the dancers were long-legged and beautiful and all kicked head-high in precision lock step to the beat of the marching jazz band that followed them. The band was tearing off a show-stopping arrangement of "I Got Rhythm."

Jeremy was a tiny bit irked by all this. "Hey. This is gettin' weird. I mean, *really* weird."

"You mean weirder than usual."

"Yeah."

They stood well aside to let the chorus line pass, then began walking the other way as the band marched by in threes. Music echoed down the hallway.

"Does all this have something to do with the party?" Jeremy asked.

"Sheila's party is over, as far as I know."

"Got any idea what's going on?"

"Not a clue."

"Well, I'm going up to the lab. Maybe the instruments show something."

"I'll go with you."

They turned left at the next intersecting corridor, but soon saw that the way ahead was blocked. Another chorus line and jazz band were kicking their way forward, but wriggling beside them was a file of belly dancers.

"Oops," Melanie said.

"In here."

They ducked into a formal sitting room, cut across it, and came out into another hallway.

But here there was something different. Minstrels.

"Oh, my," Melanie said.

"Can you play that thing, fair maid?"

The man who spoke was tall and smiling and dark-haired, all decked out in green, a white feather sprouting from his cap. He was very handsome, and Melanie fell instantly in love.

"Uh, yes," she said. "Sure. A little, anyway."

The man began to play, his three companions backing him up.

He sang:

> *"True Thomas lay on Huntly Bank*
> *A wonder he spied, spied he;*
> *For there he saw a lady bright*
> *Come riding down by the Eildon Tree . . ."*

Melanie tried to play along. The chord structure they followed was a little complex for her, but she began to enjoy the effort.

"Hey, Melanie?" Jeremy called, trying to get her attention.

Was that a minor chord there, or a diminished?

"Melanie?"

"Huh?"

"Come on, let's go."

"Oh. Can you wait just a sec?"

The troubadours stopped and the lead singer said, "That was splendid, girl! How would you like to join us? We'll travel together, eat together, sing together. It will be marvelous!"

Melanie was nonplused. "Oh, well, that's nice of you, but—"

The singer strummed a chord on his lute.

> *"Come live with me and be my love*
> *And we shall all the pleasures prove—"*

"Hey, Melanie, forget this goof. Come on."

"Wait a minute, Jeremy. Look, it would be nice and all—I mean, you guys are really good. . . ."

> *"And we will sit upon the rocks,*
> *Seeing the shepherds feed their flocks,*
> *By shallow rivers to whose falls*
> *Melodious birds sing madrigals."*

"Melanie, they aren't real."

Melanie turned her head to Jeremy.

"What?"

"They aren't real," Jeremy told her. "Can't you see that?"

The singer stopped. "Who's to say who's real, young man? You can join us, too. Some of us like boys now and then."

The minstrels all laughed.

"Come on, Melanie." Jeremy tugged at her arm.

"Hold on a second, Jeremy." She turned back to the handsome singer. "Uh, what's your name?"

The singer shrugged. "What's in a name? Call me what you like."

"You don't have a name?"

"I've never had the need—"

Everyone's attention was diverted by the approach of another band of medieval musicians. Melanie turned to look, and her eyes bulged. She looked back at the first bunch, then swung to the new arrivals.

They were identical.

"Fair maid, can you play that thing?"

Melanie slapped her forehead. "Jeremy, you're right. I should have known."

"Then let's get out of here."

Melanie and Jeremy circled past the originals and headed down the hall.

"Fare thee well, beautiful maid!"

"Uh . . . 'Bye!" Melanie called over her shoulder.

Rats. If only he wasn't so damned good-looking!

"And I will make thee beds of roses
And a thousand fragrant posies . . ."

Queen's Ladies' Quilting Room

Snowclaw.

He of the ice-white claws and fierce yellow eyes—a mountain of a beast in arctic fur as white as the driven snow.

"Snowy."

"Big Guy."

"The Snowster!"

These were, among his human friends, but a few of his sobriquets. Nevertheless, many a human had run at the sight of him. And no wonder, for he was a fearsome beast.

He stepped out of the magic doorway linking his home world to the castle and found himself confronted with quilts at every turn; quilts, garishly multicolored quilts, draping the walls and lending the room an air of comfortable coziness.

He hated it.

He was an intelligent beast; therefore he knew that his doorway had shifted position in the castle. But no matter. As long as he was in the castle. And he was. He sniffed. He could smell it.

He strode out of the room and down the hall. At the

corner he turned right, walked the length of the passageway, turned left, and hiked past several sitting rooms, a banquet hall, a meeting room, a parlor (in Victorian decor), and a ballet studio (mostly used for aerobics).

Right. He knew where he was now.

There seemed to be a lot going on. He heard noises. In passing, he glanced down a few crossing corridors and saw much activity.

A few groups of humans in fancy dress passed going the other way. Humans were always dressing to kill.

Clothes. Who needed them? Not when you had a thick silky pelt like Snowclaw's.

More humans. Dancing! Females, mostly. He paid them no mind. He heard noise that he knew to be "music." Awful stuff. He hated it. But he had heard worse.

A few more turns brought him to a hallway lined with bedroom doors. He stopped at the third one on the right, turned the handle, and went in.

There were creatures in his room. They were sweeping the floor.

He looked them over. Little fellows. Vaguely human. Fine. It was all right. Someone came in to sweep up occasionally. Not often, but occasionally. (Only the bravest chambermaids went near the place, along with the odd pageboy who had no fear.)

He had thrown out most of the furniture. For a bed he had substituted a pile of furs, comfortably strewn about with gnawed bones.

He had eaten the nightstand one evening after waking up hungry.

The wardrobe he had not consumed, for in it he kept his trusty weapon: a huge broadaxe, its wicked blade oiled and gleaming. He opened the door and took the deadly thing out.

After swishing it about a few times, he slung it over his shoulder.

Now he felt ready to face anything. In fact, he was itching to get into a fight or two. Hadn't been in a dust-up in . . . oh, must be two lunations. No, three. More, possibly.

He looked at the little fellows again. Still doing their job. "Hey!"

They paid no attention to him.

"Leave those bones in a pile there. Right there."

They were pushing all the dirt and stuff into little piles. Well, they could keep the dirt. But those bones came in handy as snacks.

"You're doing a good job, guys."

He strode out of the room, leaving the door open.

He encountered more humans, and these sang as well as danced. The males carried black canes and wore black suits and black cylindrical hats, and the females wore little. The males picked the females up and threw them around. More music played. Well, good.

More dancers. More singers. There certainly was a great deal going on around here. But there usually was. Humans. You had to like 'em, they were so interesting.

Snowclaw was hungry. This also was nothing unusual; he was in a perpetual state of being ravenous, some stages more acute than others. He sniffed and snorted, smelling human food.

He hated human food.

Well, not really. He'd eat it in a pinch. And this was such a pinch.

A male human, unknown to him, stepped up. Dressed in a loud sports coat, he was fat and bald and had a sad face. Snowclaw halted.

"I'm telling you it's murder," the man said. "I never get

invited to parties. Last time I got invited to a party I bought a hundred bucks' worth of Tupperware. I don't have any luck at all, none at all. I have to crash parties. Last one I crashed turned out to be an A.A. meeting. They threw me out. Said they couldn't stand drunks.''

Snowclaw said, ''Right.'' He strode on.

''I never have any luck, no luck at all,'' the man called after him.

Snowclaw turned left and met up with a huge animal. It was four-legged and hairless, with baggy gray skin, wide round hooves, big floppy ears, a tiny tail, and a long prehensile proboscis. A pretty female human rode high on its back.

''Right,'' Snowclaw said.

A procession of these creatures lumbered past, leaving in its wake a string of odoriferous punctuation, deposited along the flagstones.

Farther on, he came across more dancers, these with little metal things on their shoes that made tapping sounds on the floor. Then another bunch of dancers in different outfits, wearing slippers. The females spun on their toes, and, again, the males threw the females around.

The place was certainly busy today. Then again, that's the way things usually were in the castle.

He entered the dining hall. No one was about except for a lone human, drinking coffee at the end of the long table. As was the custom, the table was set with all sorts of food.

''Where is everybody?'' Snowclaw asked the man, who wore a white turban.

''They are all out trying to find the source of the disturbance.''

''Yeah? Okay. Thanks.''

Snowclaw searched the table, ignoring tureens of ox-tail

soup and plates of truffles and chafing dishes of veal Prince
Orloff, until he found what he wanted.

Beeswax candles. He liked them better than the paraffin
kind, which would do only in the tightest of pinches. He
snapped one off between his ferocious gleaming choppers.
He chewed. Not bad.

But where was the stuff to dip it in? He liked to eat
candles dipped in Thousand Island dressing.

He searched the table again, to no avail. No Thousand
Island dressing.

"Now, that's odd," Snowclaw said.

CELLAR

THE STORAGE ROOM HAD INCREASED again in size. It was now a capacious chamber in a grand palace.

The place was resplendent. Colorful, voluptuous frescoes covered the walls; palm fronds drooped from hanging gardens. Water splashed happily in a dozen fountains. Exotic birds preened and fluttered in their gilded cages, filling the air with delightful song.

Everywhere was the glint of gold, the sheen of fine marble.

Eunuchs stood guard between high columns with flower-petal capitals. Exquisite tapestries hung from the ceiling; fine rugs of intricate design adorned the walls and cushioned the marble stairways.

The main floor, a vast expanse of travertine, was filled with dancers, singers, musicians, and entertainers of every stripe: animal acts, acrobats, jugglers . . . and so forth and so on—hundreds, perhaps thousands of them, leaping and somersaulting and vocalizing and running in circles. Elephants trumpeted, dogs yipped and walked on hind legs.

Sword swallowers consumed their wares, fire-eaters ate and spat flame.

Comedians of every sort cavorted: clowns, harlequins, midgets, grotesques, slapping and kicking and tumbling and goosing.

All this activity raised quite a din, making it difficult if not impossible to hear any of the twenty-seven orchestras; nevertheless, these played doggedly on.

The immense chamber had several levels, and on a dais above the main floor two potentates reigned supreme over the proceedings. They were attended by scores of female servants, most of whom wore little or nothing at all.

King Thorsby rose on one elbow and stared glassy-eyed at the throng on the floor below. He was very drunk.

"Wh . . . whassat?"

"Pardon, Your Greatness?"

"I said, wha's all that . . . ?" He belched, then waved his arm vaguely. "Out there."

"The entertainment, Great One."

"Oh. That's still going on?"

"It will go on as long as you wish, master and lord."

"Well, it's . . ." A great belch again escaped him. "Blast. It's grown a bit hoary, it has."

"Master?"

"It's *boring*. Do something else."

"We will do anything you wish, Great King and Ruler."

"Splendid. I need a drink."

A drink was offered. Thorsby took a long draught.

"And what is your wish, master?"

Thorsby wiped his mouth on the sleeve of his satin toga. "Eh?"

"What is my master's wish?"

"I'll bite. Oh, my wish. Yes, well . . . let me see. Uh, Fetchen? Fetchen, old boy."

Fetchen surfaced from under a sea of bodies. His lips were stained purple, his face smeared with pulp and juice.

Thorsby's eyebrows arched. "Whatever are you doing down there?"

"We're having a fruit-eating contest."

"Jolly good. I say, Fetchen, old boy, what do you fancy in the way of further diversion?"

"I've about got my hands full."

"Understood, old darling, but all this lot needs something to occupy their time."

Fetchen tilted a wineskin into the ripe air and drank. Done, mouth scrubbed on a nearby thigh, he said, "Let's have gladiators."

Thorsby brightened. "Capital idea! Splendid thinking, old darling. Yes, nothing like a bit of blood sport to set the old ticker racing. Right! You heard His Imperial Decadence. Let the games begin!"

The attending houris chorused: "Let the games begin!"

And indeed they did.

KEEP—HIGH TOWER

CARRYING THREE SACKS of gold and jewels, Kwip climbed the spiral stairs of the High Tower, huffing and puffing. He was hating every minute of it.

Trying to get away from the confusion on the lower levels of the keep, he had first tried to reach the basement, only to find that the strange apparitions increased the lower he went. He had run to the nearest tower and begun climbing. He had been climbing steadily for the better part of an hour.

The High Tower was high indeed. But was it high enough?

Periodically he had stopped to explore a floor or two, finding more anomalies, more odd goings-on. Harlequins and troubadours milling about. Marching orchestras playing their ''music'' at unbelievable volume. How anyone could abide such noise was beyond his comprehension.

No matter. He would hole up somewhere, hie himself through an aspect and fritter away some time there until the tumult died down.

But you never knew about aspects. You didn't want to go blundering into one without reconnoitering. And loaded as he was with swag?—well, that was taking an enormous risk. He hoped to avoid risk altogether. The castle was a vasty barn; surely it was big enough to provide a hiding place. Surely the hurly-burly wouldn't spread to the entire castle.

Someone was coming down the stairs.

He suppressed an impulse to run back down. Better to brass it out.

A youngish man with a thin, scratchy-looking beard came round the bend of the stairwell. He was dressed in a slovenly T-shirt and faded jeans. Seeing Kwip, he halted.

"Did you ever wonder why the next line over in a bank moves faster than yours? And when you get in that line, the line you were in starts to move faster? That happens in supermarkets, too. Did you ever wonder about that?"

Kwip kept silent and continued marching up the steps.

"And did you ever notice that the lane you're driving in always ends in five hundred feet? It's never the other lane! Why is that?"

Kwip passed him and kept climbing.

The comedian didn't follow but kept on talking.

"Why can't you be 'unkempt' but you can't be 'kempt'? How can you be un-something but you can't be the something? That's not logical. And did you ever wonder about—?"

"Blow it out your arsehole!" Kwip growled over his shoulder.

He kept mounting the stair, the sacks growing heavier and heavier. He was exhausted. He couldn't climb another flight. When he reached the next landing, he exited the stairwell.

"Gods!"

More pandemonium. Here were hallways choked with buskers, circus acts, ballet troupes, and vaudeville dance-and-patter teams. A juggler juggling muskmelons walked past. A trained seal flippered by, a huge beach ball balanced on its snout.

"Ye gods and green salamanders."

Kwip steeled himself, resettled the bags against his back, and struck out into the melee.

"I don't have any luck at all," a stocky man complained in passing. "I'm tellin' you, it's murder."

Kwip moved on.

Turning a corner, he halted in his tracks. Lions!

And a lion-tamer in jodhpurs and riding boots, whip in hand. There came a cracking and much roaring.

Kwip backstepped hastily.

He found another crossing corridor, this one relatively empty, and lit out into it. He proceeded cautiously. The din of all the huggermugger echoed in his ears, and the smell of animal dung assailed his nostrils. Shouts and commotion came from every quarter.

He wondered, *What in the name of all the gods is going on?* The castle had never been like this in all his experience of it. It was ofttimes a place fit for madmen, true enough; but its madness had never reached such a fever pitch. This was sheerest insanity. What lay behind it all? Witchery, he guessed. Evil spells. What else? Such was the cause of most of the trouble around here. Find a fracas, turn over the bodies, and you'd doubtless reveal one kind of magical trickery or another. The place was rife with sorcerers. Sometimes he had half a mind to quit it all, rush pell-mell through the first aspect that presented itself, and the devil take the hindmost!

A great maned lion came round the corner ahead. It stopped in its tracks and glowered at Kwip.

Kwip halted. He smiled weakly.

"Nice puss," he said.

The lion snarled. Then it sniffed. Fresh meat.

"N-n . . ." Kwip licked his dry lips and swallowed. "Nice pussy. Dear pussycat." He began to back off.

The lion advanced a few steps forward, still taking Kwip's olfactory measure. Its tail swished back and forth.

Kwip hurled the sacks at it and ran. At his back, the lion roared.

Out of the corner of his eye he caught sight of trees and blue sky. An aspect! He altered his path and ran for it, crossing through an alcove. He streaked through the magic doorway. Into another world.

Coming out into fresh air, he sprinted across a grassy clearing. On reaching its other side he dove into low brush, hunkered down low, and held his breath.

He pushed a twig aside and looked out. The clearing was empty. The lion hadn't followed.

He exhaled and took off his cap, wiped his brow with his sleeve. Ye gods.

Ye gods! The gold! He'd left it strewn across the castle flagstones. He'd best get back there quickly.

He looked again. No great beasts in sight. But there was plenty of cover to hide a big cat. He didn't want to risk being caught out in the open. He'd better wait a bit.

But all he could think of was the gold. Glittering yellow metal, finely wrought into cups and plates and medallions and rings and things, all scattered about the castle, waiting for the first person to come along and scoop them up. Blast! It was likely all gone already! Where was that infernal beast?

He peered out once more. Nothing. He'd have to risk it. Now, where was the portal? There.

No. There. No, wrong again. It should be directly across the clearing. The grass wasn't tall enough to have bent in his path; no tracks to retrace his steps. But he hadn't run that far. The way back to the castle should be . . . there.

Well, it was somewhere about, of that he was sure. With no lion to bother him, he would simply search until he found it. Unless . . .

Unless this was an aspect that tended to pop in and out of existence, as some were wont to do. In that case, the portal might have disappeared, and he'd be stranded. Best not to think of that, yet.

He put on his cap. He got to his feet slowly, looking around, then cautiously came out from cover. He began to walk back across the clearing.

He was halfway across when a tremendous explosion threw up great gouts of earth at the far end of the clearing. The concussion knocked him down, and clods of dirt rained down on him.

He was dazed, but was almost to his feet when another explosion hit in the woods he'd just left, to the same effect. More shocks followed.

He staggered for the tree line, and when he reached it, the portal was not to be found. He fell behind a bush, lay flat, and covered his head with his arms.

A salvo of artillery shells hit the clearing, shaking the earth and engendering in Kwip's benumbed mind the consoling thought that he didn't have to worry about the gold.

He would never see the castle again.

PIRAEON

THE ASSEMBLED ARMADA CHOKED THE HARBOR. There were almost four hundred ships, hailing from all over Arkadia, its possessions, protectorates, fiefdoms, and allies. Ships of every class lay moored to the docks and anchored as far out as the breakwaters: sailing vessels, galleys, longboats—even a few barges. A good number were warships of Arkadian design—long, sleek galleys-cum-sail with high curved sterns and sharp low ramming-prows. But there were also modified traders, refitted fishing boats, and other improvisations. They'd scoured every harbor in the Central Sea to get this show together.

Trent sat at a table in front of his tent, which had been pitched on the leeward side of the hill above the harbor. He was trying to get some food into him. After what was going to happen in a very short while, he knew his appetite would vanish.

It was practically gone already. He had before him a very good ripened cheese from Tyras, a fine red Megaran wine, raw chopped lamb with olive oil, shallots and garlic, and good local bread; but he was barely able to force anything down. Nevertheless, he cut himself another wedge of cheese.

His young servant, Strephon, offered him more wine. That he could handle.

"Thank you," Trent said.

Strephon bowed and went back into the tent.

Trent downed the wine, wiped his mouth on his sleeve. He pushed the cheese away.

No, food didn't go well with human sacrifice.

He looked up at the sky. It had been overcast for three solid weeks, the fierce winds bringing one storm after another. It was, he'd been told, the worst weather for this region in a century. The fleet had twice essayed a crossing of the Therean Sea to Dardanian waters, and twice foul weather had turned it back. Anthaemion was convinced the gods were against him, and was further convinced nothing less than a supreme sacrifice would propitiate them.

How did he know? He had been told so in a dream.

A frigging dream. Can you beat that?

Say, let's kill somebody. Why? Well, I had this dream, see. . . .

Right.

Trent sighed. No use condemning these benighted people. These were archaic, god-ridden times, centuries before the light of reason would dawn—if it ever would. (He had to keep reminding himself that this was not Earth and history did not have to unfold the way it did on Earth.) They didn't know any better; superstition was a way of life. Gods spoke in dreams, through oracles, out of the mouths of priests. If the gods demanded blood (and he also had to keep reminding himself that human sacrifice was fairly rare here), they got blood. Most of the time they were satisfied with a bit of roast lamb. But every once in a while they got a hankering for more exotic fare.

Damn. Trent drank more of the excellent wine. It was a little like a Valpolicella. Not much, but a little.

The thing that most upset him was that he couldn't do anything to prevent it. He had tried. He had talked, reasoned, argued, and cajoled until he was blue in the face. To no avail. Anthaemion remained adamant that nothing less than the sacrifice of his own daughter would ameliorate the wrath of those gods who had set themselves against the cause of the Arkadians.

Well, maybe she was his daughter. She was the daughter of one of his concubines, but it was common knowledge that they slept around. Anthaemion might not be the girl's father. He probably hadn't even known her name up until a day or so ago.

So maybe she wasn't his daughter. What difference did that make? That didn't make the cheese go down any easier. It didn't assuage Trent's vague sense of responsibility for having failed to talk Anthaemion out of it. The king had been on the verge of changing his mind several times, Trent had felt. If only he had pursued a point better, or presented something more to advantage, or tricked up some clever argument—

No, no use. He'd tried his best, and he'd failed. It was as simple as that.

And what did it matter, finally, to him? This was not his land, these were not his times—this was not his *world*, for pity's sake. He wished his conscience would leave him alone.

Telamon was coming up the hill. Trent rose, forced a smile, and waved.

The Chamberlain waved back and returned the smile briefly. He mounted the last rise to the terrace slowly, hale fellow though he was. It was steep, this path up to the acropolis and its temples. Trent had ordered his tent pitched up here to get above the rotten-fish smell of the port city, to take advantage of the shelter provided by the lee side of the hill, and most of all to get away from the constant brawls and killings among the Arkadian hosts below. Ten thousand idle, itchy sword hands made for a nervous bivouac. Even at the best of times, Arkadians were a vendetta-plagued, murderous lot.

They were human beings. So what else was new?

Telamon looked grim.

"Hail, Trent."

"Telamon. Have you eaten?"

"Yes. A swallow of wine, however."

Pouring, Trent said, "Sit, drink."

Telamon did so as Trent called for another cup, which Strephon soon delivered.

Telamon looked up. "No break in the weather."

Trent followed his gaze to the leaden grayness above. "No. Another storm is predicted." Trent took a drink and looked at the Chamberlain. "Is Anthaemion determined to do the thing?"

Telamon nodded gravely. "He is. They'll be up in a trice with the girl."

"Gods. How young . . . ?" Trent shook his head. "No, I don't want to know."

"Best not to think of anything now but our duty."

Trent said nothing. He wanted to tell Telamon that they were all crazy. He didn't, of course.

"The gods are strange in their ways," Telamon mused, watching fast gray clouds chase across the sky. "They are capricious. They are sometimes cruel. Yet they are gods, and we must accept them as they are and obey their will."

"Yes, of course," Trent said. "But all we know is that the king had a dream. We do not know the will of the gods."

"But they have not shown any sign that they do not want this thing done."

"What would such a sign consist of?"

"I cannot say. But surely they would make their displeasure known in some way. They always do."

Trent heaved an internal sigh. You simply couldn't argue with these people. No way to undercut their assumptions. But how did they know the king's dream came from a god? Well, he was the king, wasn't he? Q.E.D.

Trent began to construct another counterargument, but gave it up. There was nothing he could say to stop the killing. The only alternative was to use his magic.

But that involved another hitch. Several. For one, this world was very flat, magically speaking. Meaning that it was hard to work any here. It could be done, with some effort, but each world's magic was different, and Trent hadn't had much time to delve into the working of the Arts here. Consequently, his repertoire was limited. For another, these people were very sensitive to magical goings-on. No doubt Anthaemion would detect meddling. He wouldn't like it a bit, and would instantly suspect Trent.

That would never do.

There was still another consideration. Inky had explicitly told him to lay off. His role here was limited to that of a military adviser. He was not supposed to use magic except in a military situation, and, in that case, nothing more than a temporary invisibility spell or two. If that. In fact, Trent had not planned to use any supernatural crutches at all. Tricks would only complicate the situation; besides, military magic was not always effective. Better to keep your power dry and your sword sharp. Rely on hocus-pocus at your peril.

So, the upshot: mind your own gods-damned business.

Telamon talked of other things while Trent's mind

wandered. He wondered about Sheila and exactly how long he'd been gone now, according to Sheila's sense of time. He suspected that Inky had misrepresented the time-flow variance. Damn him.

Trent was worried, because in this world, this universe, three solid months had passed since he'd arrived. He hoped Sheila wasn't fretting. Inky had assured him he'd get word to her in case of any undue delay in his return. But how much time? How long was his absence, reckoning by castle-time: A day? A week? Perhaps as much as a month had gone by. Sheila would be beside herself.

But he was committed. He couldn't pull out. He'd pledged his help and he had to follow through. A matter of his word, his honor.

"You are distracted, friend," Telamon was saying.

"Hm? Oh, sorry. Yes, I'm afraid I can't get my mind off this business. I really wish—"

Telamon looked down at the slope. "It will be over soon, and there will be no more to think about."

Trent looked. A procession was coming up the path. Anthaemion, his court, his palace guard, others. And two soldiers escorting a young woman.

God, she looks all of fourteen, Trent said to himself.

He downed the last of his wine and rose with Telamon. They waited.

The procession wound up the stone path. As it passed, he watched the girl. She wore a garland of myrtle around her head and was dressed in white robes. She was young, much too young. How could that miserable swine do such a thing?

She turned her head and looked at Trent. A faint smile crept across her lips. Bashfully, she turned her head away.

She didn't know! And wouldn't till the last second, he hoped. Thank the gods.

He'd better stop using that expression. These weren't his gods. If they existed. Not that he had really ever . . .

Never mind, never mind. Should he go up and witness the bloody thing? Or stay here and get drunk, and a pox on the whole bunch of irrational, superstitious bastards?

The procession passed. He and Telamon followed it up the slope.

Trent's mind churned all the way up.

The temple complex on the acropolis was small. Three temples, but only one was anything more than a gazebo affair. There were a few other small buildings and shrines. The procession passed all these and headed for the open-air altar, a stepped pyramid that sat on the edge of a cliff above the sea.

Clouds of darker gray gathered above. The buildings were made of white marble, but they were old and weathered, even in this ancient time. (But now is now, Trent thought, correcting himself once again. *And this is not Earth*.)

Trent didn't know what gods or goddesses any of these structures were dedicated to, nor did he care.

On the altar's highest level sat a stone brazier, good for barbecues and your basic holocaust. Kill the victim, then burn the remains. That was how it was done. Usually the victim was not human.

Trent lost sight of the head of the procession. He broke into a run to catch up.

He sidestepped, ducked, and pushed his way through the clot of soldiers, sailors, courtiers, and noblemen, leaving ruffled dignity in his wake. Nasty looks were thrown his way, and a few swords came halfway out of scabbards. But he elbowed his way forward.

He reached the first step of the altar and began to climb,

but hit an impasse. Bodies blocked his way. He lunged. One man fell over backwards. He gained two steps. Curses came to his ears from behind.

"Foreign trash!"

"Sorcerous dog!"

And worse, but he paid it no mind. Most were reluctant to challenge a sorcerer. He kept pushing his way up the terraced altar.

One ornery soldier wasn't about to let him pass. Snarling, the man drew his sword. Trent kneed him in the balls.

He pushed upward. Finally, he was at the top, but more noble carcasses barred his way.

He heard the girl scream. He jabbed his fist into the spine of the man in front of him.

When he went down Trent broke into the clear, and stopped in his tracks.

Above him, on the highest stone platform, Anthaemion stood with his right arm upraised, the gold of his bronze blade against the gray sky, ready to bring it down on the terrified child. The king's eyes were dark, a kind of resolute fury in them. Though he hesitated, he was clearly determined to see this through.

A blinding flash lit up the acropolis.

The blade of the king's sword was the focal point. Spider-legs of blue fire crawled from it, metastasizing to a circle of points around the oval brazier. A blue glow enveloped everyone and everything. Simultaneously, one of the spider-legs darted to Trent, lifted him up, and hurled him over the heads of the crowd. Then a cascade of sparks radiated from the king's sword, and white smoke rose from it.

A tremendous crash resounded. People tumbled over each other down the steps.

The sea echoed thunder.

* * *

Telamon's face came into focus.

"Trent?"

Trent raised his head.

"What happened?" he asked.

"The sign."

"Uh, yeah."

Telamon helped Trent sit up, then palpated his arms, his legs, all of him. Nothing broken. Trent tried to get up, found that he could.

"The gods have spoken," Telamon said, "as they always do."

"Loud and clear," Trent said. He was a little dazed, and his ears hurt. He turned to find Anthaemion looking at him.

The crowd had dispersed. A few lingered to stare at the top of the altar.

"Come with me," Anthaemion commanded.

Trent followed him back to the top of the altar. There, the king stopped and looked down at something lying at his feet: a piece of twisted half-fused metal.

Trent looked. It was Anthaemion's sword.

"It was a trial, a test," the king of Mykos said, staring at the thing.

"Yes," Trent said.

"To see if I would obey. And I obeyed."

"Yes," Trent said again. He had command of few words at the moment. "The girl? She . . . ?"

Anthaemion looked at Trent. "She is unhurt."

"Ah."

"You were right, Trent. But the gods had their plan, which you tried to thwart. And I had no choice. Now, the gods have seen to it that my conscience is clear."

Trent nodded.

Anthaemion took a long breath. "I felt nothing," he said.

"The lightning's fire passed through me. Yet I had no sensation. Was there much pain for you?"

"Nothing at all," Trent told him.

Anthaemion nodded. "The gods are all-powerful. And all-wise." He looked out over the cliff. "We cannot fail now."

"No. I suppose not."

Trent went down, leaving the graying king to stare at the wine-dark sea.

Walking back down the stony path, Trent began to chuckle.

Yep. He'd played the ace about as cagily as it could be played. Anthaemion didn't suspect a thing. Close, though. Close.

Just how do you go about calling down a bolt from the sky and directing a convincing portion of it at yourself without hurting anybody or turning your carcass into a piece of charred meat?

Carefully. Very carefully.

Above the bustling seaport, a patch of blue was showing.

CASTLE KEEP—LOWER LEVELS,
NEAR THE GRAND BALLROOM

GENE WAS DRESSED FOR TROUBLE. He had on a chain-mail hood over a padded jupon (more or less a long-sleeved doublet), tights, and anachronistic high leather boots. He was packing a long broadsword and a dagger.

Linda was in leather shorts over black tights, high green felt boots, and a ruffled blouse under a leather jerkin. The scabbard of her dagger was gilded in filigree.

They had found an unoccupied sitting room and were hiding out, taking a breather, while all around them the disturbance continued. Cacophony reigned. Hundreds of orchestras clashed in disharmony while thousands of dancers and singers contributed to the din.

"I'm bushed," Gene said, collapsing on the couch.

"Yeah." Linda plopped next to him.

Gene watched a military band march past the archway, then said, "How many floors did we cover?"

"Dozen or two."

"What floor is this?"

"The sixth, I think."

"That far down? It's getting pretty congested. Think we can make it to the basement?"

"That's where the ruckus started, you said."

"I was just guessing, but judging from the fact that it gets worse the farther down we go, I'd say I was right."

"So, we go to the basement and see what's up."

"Check. As soon as I catch my second wind."

"My third."

"Oh, no."

A marching band in green uniforms with gold piping and epaulets trooped through the room, blaring out a peppy double-time number. Linda covered her ears and buried her face in the sofa.

When the last piccolo player had fast-stepped out, Gene said, "I wonder where the football game is."

"God, they were *loud*," Linda complained as she sat up.

"Maybe this isn't the most dangerous disturbance we've had at the castle, but it certainly is the most annoying. What a racket."

"I wish there was a door to this place."

Gene looked at her, frowning.

She returned his stare. "What are you—?" Then it dawned on her. "Oh. Yeah, right."

She folded her arms and twitched her nose.

A stout oak door appeared under the formerly open archway to their right, along with a fitted section of wall. When she twitched again, an identical assemblage materialized to block the entrance opposite. The din outside became a dull hum.

"Sorry," she said. "Should have thought of it."

"That nose business you do is strangely evocative, I must say."

"I've rigged it as a trigger for my spells. I stole it from an old TV sitcom."

"Of course. Television, the source of all wisdom. I'll never live up to Darin."

"Of course you will. Who'll play the mother-in-law?"

"Endora? Deena."

"Great, we're set for a long season."

"High ratings."

They laughed, then fell silent.

At length Linda said, "Sure is quiet."

"Yup."

She looked at Gene. "Want to talk about it?"

"It? Oh."

"Us?"

"Yeah, us. What about us?"

She shrugged. "Any future?"

He shrugged in turn. "Dunno."

"Should we have an affair?"

Gene chuckled. "What a question."

"I'm serious."

"You really want my opinion?"

"Yes."

"No."

"We shouldn't?"

"Probably not," Gene said. "We make a good team. We've gone through a lot together. Maybe we shouldn't complicate it."

Linda's shoulders fell a little. "Maybe not."

"Are you relieved or disappointed?"

"Don't know, really."

"Are you hurt?"

"Hurt? No, not at all."

"I like you, Linda."

"And I like you. Guess I was being silly."

"No. Oh, hell. Linda, I think you're attractive."

"You do? You've never said so."

"No, guess I never have said so. Seems to me that the subject simply never came up. But it's true. I've always thought you were attractive. The thing is . . ."

"What?"

"I've always thought of you as . . . above it all."

"Above what?"

"You've always seemed . . . What am I trying to say? Uninterested, aloof from anything so mundane as romance."

"Really?" Linda was amazed.

"Not true?"

Linda thought about it. "Call it hibernation. I was just in a dormant state. You're forgetting the psychological wreck I was when I arrived here."

Gene thought back. "You're right. I'd quite forgot."

"So now maybe I'm better. Or thought I was. Ready for romance. But that's out of the question."

"Hey, I never said it was out of the question."

"What did you say?"

"Well, you asked me if I thought it was a good idea for us to . . . you know."

Linda smiled. "You know?"

"You know, do that thing."

"Sleep together. Gene, you're almost blushing."

"Don't be silly, my dear. We men of the world—"

"You are blushing! You must have taken up with a dozen women since I've known you."

"What? You're dreaming! And as far as blushing is concerned, I'm blushing because you're trying to make me blush. Stop that!"

Linda giggled. "Sorry."

"Okay, well . . . What the hell were we talking about?"

"Having sex."

"Good God, woman! This isn't a proper conversation, not at all, not at all."

"Prude."

"Besides, 'sex' in that usage is a misnomer, you know. 'Sex' means gender, not coitus."

"You should go on *Jeopardy.*"

"Well, it's true."

"Fine. Anyway. So you didn't rule it out, but you don't think we should."

"That's more or less what I said."

Linda nodded. "Okay, I can live with that, I suppose."

"Wait a minute. What do *you* think?"

"What's it matter what I think if you don't think it's a good idea?"

"Because the fact that it might not be—I say *might* not be—such a good idea doesn't have anything to do with my maybe wanting to do it."

"So your answer is maybe?"

Gene crossed his ankles and leaned back. "Maybe."

"Your answer is maybe, or maybe your answer is maybe?"

"It may be that maybe is my answer."

"God, talk about playing hard to get."

"Who's playing hard to get? All I said was—"

"You said maybe maybe."

"Maybe maybe?"

"Not just one maybe. Double maybe."

"No, what I said was—"

"I don't believe this," Linda said. "The *woman* is supposed to play hard to get."

"Well, these are the nineties. The gay nineties."

"Don't be silly. Maybe you're right, though."

"Right about what?" Gene asked.

"About us not being compatible."

"I didn't say that."

"You didn't? But you said we'd be no good together. Maybe that's true. For one thing, you're six times brighter than I am."

"Oh, please."

"No, really. Sometimes you're so bright you blind me. You're witty and charming. You're absolute greased lightning with a comeback, and you always know the right thing to say—"

"Give me a freaking break."

"Listen to me. Sometimes I can't keep up with you."

"You listen to me," Gene told her. "One of the reasons I like having you around is that you let me *be* bright and charming and oh-so witty. People are different depending on who they're with, you know. If I'm charming when you're around, it's only because you bring that out in me."

Linda looked at him for a moment before she said, "That's a nice thing to say."

"It's true."

"Thank you for saying it. But you do intimidate me sometimes."

"Sorry, don't mean to."

"I know it's not intentional."

"Last thing I want to do is intimidate you. Some other people, yes. So, you think this is major problem between us?"

Linda shook her head. "No, I'm not saying it's a major problem."

"A minor problem?"

"Uh, well, maybe."

Gene said, "Lots of maybes in this conversation."

"Yeah. Seriously, I don't want to give the impression that I think there are these major barriers between us. Just . . . well, what I'm saying is . . . uh . . ."

"What are you saying?"

"What are *you* saying?"

"What I said."

"Which was?"

Gene thought about it. "I need to think about this a little bit more."

"There's hope?"

"Are you hoping there's hope?"

"Are you?"

Gene laughed. "This is like a poker game."

"How so?"

"Playing close to the vest. We don't want to tip our hands."

"Maybe we're both afraid of being hurt," Linda said.

"Maybe we're both bluffing?"

"Could be. Maybe we should leave it at that."

"More maybes."

"Yeah." Linda suddenly yawned. "Oh, excuse me."

"You want me to take a nap?"

"I'd love to."

The noise level jumped and startled them both.

Gene glanced at both entrances. The magically created doors were gone.

"You're doing your disappearing act well these days," he commented.

"I don't make anything disappear," she said. "I just make the spell weak, and when it fizzles, the thing I conjured just vanishes."

"Oh, is that how you do it? Neat. You want to rest more?"

"No, let's get to the bottom of this. We have to."

"Okay. But I hate to—"

A large, well-muscled man came bursting through the archway. He wore the visored steel helmet and greaves of a gladiator and carried a shield, but his chest was vulnerably bare. Seeing Gene, he raised his short-sword and charged.

Gene leaped up and drew in time to parry the man's lunging thrust. Stepping deftly aside, he tripped his assailant and laid the flat of his sword sharply across the man's bare back.

The man yelled and went tumbling. But he was quick to recover, get to his feet, and charge again.

Gene and the gladiator fought. The shield was an advantage, but Gene was by far the abler swordsman. In short order Gene had the man backed into a corner, and slashing two-handed with his larger and superior weapon, reduced the shield to a battered and dented plate.

Linda, watching from behind the couch, let out a tiny scream when Gene found an opening and thrust his sword home.

Grimacing, the man dropped both shield and sword to grasp the blade that had buried itself deep in his abdomen.

"Thou hast conquered, comrade," he gasped.

Gene withdrew the bloodied blade as the man fell. The gladiator drew one last breath.

Then he disappeared.

"That's a relief," Gene said, looking at his sword, which was no longer bloody. "Didn't think he was real, but he sure put on a good show."

"Gene, if he'd killed you . . ."

"*Morituri te salutamus.* I sure as hell wouldn't disappear. I'd stay right there, deader 'n a doorstop."

Two more gladiators spilled into the sitting room, swords clashing, shields banging. Gene ran and leaped over the couch.

"We'd better get out of here," he told Linda.

Another pair of fighters, engaged in mortal combat, came

in through the opposite entrance. Both pairs ignored Gene and Linda, who began backing out of the room.

"As long as there's an even number of combatants," Gene observed, "we won't be attacked. But the loose guys are going to be a problem."

"Do you want to head back up?"

Gene shook his head. "No, my sword magic gives me the advantage. We have to see what's behind all this. You want to hide out somewhere while I go below?"

"Of course not. I want to be with you."

"Right. We do make a great team."

She took his hand. "Let's go, teammate," she said, leading him cautiously out into the confusion of the hall-way.

Stairwell

"What's the matter?" Dalton called back over his shoulder. "Getting winded, old boy?"

Below, Thaxton was slow to mount the next few steps. "Nothing of the kind. Just feathering back a bit to conserve strength."

"Only five more stories to the top."

"Right."

Thaxton took two steps at a time to catch up, winding his way up the spiral stairwell. But when he reached the spot where Dalton stood waiting, he wilted.

He sat and heaved a weary sigh. "Gadzooks."

"You should get more exercise, old fellow. Play a little golf now and then."

Thaxton sent a withering look upward.

"Or whatever's your pleasure," Dalton amended.

Thaxton said sarcastically, "Golf is not my pleasure, as I'm sure you know."

"Sorry. Ever been up to the roof, by the way? Or the high battlements, I should say."

"No," Thaxton said. "Have you?"

"Once. Magnificent view. Plains, snow-capped mountains. Beautiful."

"I'm sure."

"Truly. But strange, disorienting in a way."

"How so?"

"Well," Dalton said, "we know there are about eighty stories to the keep. But from outside, it doesn't look it. I mean, the castle is huge, massive. But the keep looks to be only about thirty to forty stories at its highest point. Which makes it towering compared to earthly castles, but not exactly the World Trade Center either."

"Really. Can't say I'm surprised, though."

"No, the castle does tricks with interior space."

"Indeed."

"Ready?"

"A bit longer," Thaxton begged.

"No problem."

"How old are you, Dalton, old boy?"

"I'll be sixty-six come October eleven."

"Really. I must say you're in jolly good shape for an old blighter."

"Why, thank you. Strikes me that I never asked you the same question."

"Fifty-one, old boy. Fifty-one bloody years, and I feel every one of them in every bone in my body." Thaxton looked up. "Please don't bring up exercise again."

"Never!"

Thaxton looked glum. "Some people don't age well."

"Guess not."

Hauling himself upward with great effort, Thaxton said, "Remind me again what we're doing this for."

"To see if the source of the invasion is outside the castle."

"Don't they have lookouts?"

"The lookouts were pulled from their posts when the ruckus started. Tyrene needed every reinforcement. Tyrene delegated me to go up and see if anything's out there."

"Oh. I see."

"Don't expect to see much. Looks like an interior problem. Damned castle magic gone awry, like so many times before."

"Oh, yes," Thaxton said. "So many times."

They resumed climbing the helix of the stone stairwell. Every third turn brought round an embrasured window, but the narrow aperture offered a limited view. The windows let in some daylight, however.

They had encountered anomalies on the lower levels: comedians spouting routines to anyone who'd listen, Oriental jugglers, and so forth; but the apparitions had petered out at about the sixtieth floor.

At last they came to the highest landing and a stout oak door set into the curving wall. Dalton opened it and went through, Thaxton following. They came out into brisk open air and a maze of high, windswept parapets.

"Good Lord."

There was a lot to see. First, the castle itself. They found themselves on a walkway running along the keep's battlements. The castle keep was eye-defying in its complexity, bristling with hundreds of towers. Below lay a maze of walls enclosing more walls, marking off wards and barbicans and a thousand different cloisters and courtyards. Parapets capped the walls and ramparts. Enclosing the keep itself was a concentric network of curtain-walls and bastions, each higher and more formidable than the last, until the outside wall was almost as high as the keep itself. Castle Perilous was an impregnable fortress, vast and enigmatic.

All that was left bare of the citadel on which the castle stood was a narrow ledge of rock surrounding everything. A thousand feet below that ledge lay the barren Plains of Baranthe, a snow-capped mountain range rising on its western extremity.

Gathered in all at once, it was a breathtaking view. But there was more to see.

Gossamer displays of light emanated from the keep and the entire castle. Some contained vague images: faces, human figures, various forms of animals and objects. Like auroras, these phenomena flickered and fluttered. Diaphanous birdlike images arose and flapped their way skyward before disappearing. Nothing was sharply defined; all possessed a ghostly quality.

Hovering above all this was a vague shape, gradually taking form, seeming to preside over everything. It might have been a face.

"What the devil's all this?" Thaxton wanted to know.

"Anybody's guess," Dalton said, looking up. "What do you make of that up there?"

Thaxton looked at it. "Looks like a bloke in a turban."

"Strange. Seems to be smiling at us. Unnerving."

"Yes. Uh, perhaps we should . . ."

"Definitely has something to do with what's going on in the castle," Dalton ventured. "But what, I don't know."

"Neither do I. Well, shall we be off, then?"

"Let's see what this is all about," Dalton said, venturing farther along the walkway.

"Uh . . . well, if you insist."

They walked cautiously, keeping to the middle of the walkway, Thaxton casting periodic nervous glances downward. The way was not nearly wide enough, as far as he was concerned.

"What the devil could it be?" Dalton said, eyes still on the gathering image above.

"Looks like a genie out of a bloody lamp."

"It does at that," Dalton said, stopping. "But more sinister."

"Quite. Well, the genie's loose. Let's report to Tyrene."

"It seems to be still in the process of forming. We should observe it a little."

"Yes, I suppose we should. Just a bit longer."

"Nervous?"

Thaxton feigned surprise. "Who, me, old man? Of course not. It does pay to be cautious, though."

"You're right. I don't like the looks of this. Don't like it at all."

"Yes, it does give one pause. Wish it wouldn't gawk at us like that, with that bloody insipid grin."

"Looks like it's smirking, sort of," Dalton said.

The face was a trifle more distinct now. It kept moving slightly from side to side, and continued to go in and out of focus. It looked like an image projected on a cloud of smoke. It was definitely grinning. The grin was impish, sly, and—this was quite discernible—a bit evil.

"Perhaps we should try to communicate with it," Dalton said.

"Eh? Whatever for?"

"Find out what it wants."

"Well, we know that. It wants the bloody castle. Doesn't everybody?"

Dalton cupped his hands to his mouth and yelled, "You up there? Can you hear? Can you understand?"

A sudden wind rose on the parapet. Thaxton shivered.

"Did it speak?" Dalton asked.

Thaxton said, "Pardon?"

"Did you hear it say something?"

"No, sorry."

Dalton again raised his hands to his mouth. "I say, can you hear us, whoever you are?"

Quite distinctly, came a voice from above. *No need to shout.* It was a pleasant, melodious voice, with perhaps a trace of an accent.

"Who are you?"

Laughter came from the image.

Then this, merrily: *Wouldn't you like to know?*

Dalton looked back at his partner with sardonically raised eyebrows, then turned to face the apparition. "What's your game? What do you want?"

"A Book of Verses underneath the Bough, / A Jug of Wine, a Loaf of Bread—"

"Good God, it's quoting poetry at us," Thaxton said.

"Look here," Dalton said to the thing. "We'd like to know what you're up to. You seem to be succeeding in whatever you want to accomplish. Why don't you tell us what it is?"

> *"The Moving Finger writes; and having writ,*
> *Moves on: nor all your Piety nor Wit*
> *Shall lure it back to cancel half a Line,*
> *Nor all your Tears wash out a Word of it."*

"Well, that's helpful, I must say," Thaxton sneered.

Dalton said, "Sounds like it's warning us."

"See here," Thaxton said with a finger raised. "Threats won't get you anywhere."

Again, soft laughter.

"Bet it thinks it's holding all the cards," Dalton ventured. "And maybe it is."

"Well, we're not going to get anywhere with the bloody thing, whatever it is, so we'd best—"

Dalton shouted to the skies once more: "Look here, you'd better be aware that the master of this castle is a very powerful magician. He won't take kindly to any mischief."

The laughter rose in pitch.

Thaxton cast a look behind and was dismayed. A lion, its mane shaggy and full, had just walked out of the door to the tower and was proceeding up the walkway with great interest.

Thaxton tapped his friend on the shoulder. "I say, old man . . ."

"Did you understand what I said?" Dalton continued yelling on high, his attention on the image. "His name is Incarnadine. I don't know if that name means anything to you particularly, but he's quite well-known as one of the most powerful—"

"I say, Dalton, old fellow."

"—magicians in a whole passel of worlds, so you'd best give all this business some thought before you proceed with whatever it is you're up to."

"Dalton, please, give a look behind!"

"Huh? I . . ." Dalton turned. "Holy smoke."

They ran.

The walkway made an L at the next turret and proceeded right along the battlement. The lion began loping after them, its interest piqued, but not sufficiently to induce it to give full chase. Thaxton pulled slightly ahead of Dalton, threw a wild look behind and increased his lead.

They made the circuit of a turret atop a tower that stood at an oblique-angled corner of the keep. Above, the disembodied face observed their progress with some glee. Impish laughter sounded above the rising wind.

They ran along neatly laid flagstones, past the crenelated battlements and rows of loopholes. The sun was low, throwing long shadows across the courts. The wind began to buffet them. And all around them, spectral apparitions flapped and flew, leaped and cavorted. An auroral prominence arched high into the air and dissipated, to be followed by another, not quite so spectacular but still impressive. Faint shafts of light swung like spotlight beams, crisscrossing in Hollywood-premiere flamboyance. Pink elephants and chartreuse zebras gamboled atop the revetments.

Another turret lay ahead, this one a bartizan hanging precariously far out over the wall. Thaxton ran by it but skidded to a stop on the walkway beyond.

Another lion was coming at them, from the other direction.

Dalton dashed into the turret and climbed up on the battlement.

"Thaxton, old boy! Up here. It's our only chance!"

Thaxton backed into the turret, eyeing with dismay the flanking approach of the two beasts, who had slowed their gait to a stealthy walk. He stopped and glanced behind.

"What the devil are you doing up there?"

Dalton said, "If they come any closer, we've got to lower ourselves over the side and hang on till they lose interest and go away."

"Good God, have you taken leave of your senses?"

"Maybe we won't have to. They may let us alone if we don't move."

The lions seemed determined to make a meal of it. Both had a lean and hungry look.

Thaxton said, "Oh, bloody hell."

He jumped up into the notch—crenel—adjoining the one Dalton stood on. He looked down.

"WHOOOAAAA!"

Dalton reached and grabbed him before he toppled over into empty space.

"Don't look!" Dalton commanded.

"Bloody blue blazes, how can you not look?"

"Turn around and get down on your haunches!"

Trembling and white as a ghost, Thaxton did as instructed.

"W-what now?" he wanted to know.

"We watch and see what they do."

The animals kept advancing, looking very confident that they had their prey cornered. These were not a pair of toothless old pussycats escaped from a circus; they looked quite as wild and ferocious as lions come.

"I think we had better do the hanging bit," Dalton decided.

"Can't we do something else?"

"Not unless you want to jump."

"I'm almost persuaded that would be the better course."

"Might be. But I'm for trying the other thing first."

Thaxton stiffened up a bit. "Right you are, old man. You first."

Dalton got one leg over the edge; then, grasping the inner edge of the crenel with both hands, he lowered the other leg and eased himself down.

More slowly, and with some difficulty, Thaxton did the same.

The wind gusted and tore at them. Their legs dangled over the plains.

"Oh, dear," was all Thaxton could say. His face was the color of bean curd.

Dalton's face was a grayish-green. "I'm afraid . . ." He lurched and struggled for a better handhold, his shoes scraping against the stone. "Afraid I'm losing my grip here."

Dalton's hands slipped from the inner edge of the wall. He dropped but caught himself, finding a tenuous purchase on the outer edge.

"Christ!"

Thaxton yelled, "Hang on, old boy, hang on!"

"I really think . . ."

"Here, grab onto me!"

"I'm going to fall . . ."

With great horror, Thaxton watched as his friend lost his handhold and dropped, uttering not a sound, to his certain death.

Thaxton hung there in space, the wind howling around him. Better if Dalton had screamed, he thought. All the more dreadful like that, plummeting in utter silence.

Dreadful.

LABORATORY

JEREMY STOOD PEERING at the dial of a curious device that resembled a grandfather clock, but was not a clock. It was a delicate instrument, sensitive to the ebb and flow of magic in and about the castle.

He observed the displacement of the single hand and the numeral it pointed to, then made a notation on a pad. He stepped to the next machine and did the same.

Melanie watched over his shoulder.

"These machines can tell you if something is going on?" she asked. She hadn't spent much time in the lab since coming to the castle.

"Something is going on, all right," Jeremy replied. "The question is, what is it and where is it?"

"Will those gizmos tell you that, too?"

"If I can triangulate, yeah."

"Oh."

All this didn't make much sense to Melanie. The room they were in looked like a science lab, not a place of magic. Correction: it resembled a science *fiction* lab, worthy of a chiller flick. Right out of *Frankenstein*.

Jeremy stepped to the next machine. All these unusual sensing instruments were similar, but the faces differed. Some had single hands, some had two or three, and a few had several rotating dials and gauges. All looked antique and brought to mind something one might have discovered in the study of a medieval alchemist. But no alchemist or magician had ever owned these odd contraptions. None but Incarnadine, that is.

Melanie took a self-guided tour of the lab, noting the many strange items in it, then returned. She sat at the work station of the castle's mainframe "computer." They called it a computer, but it looked like a collection of old juke boxes lost in an array of more *Frankenstein* stuff. She sat back and watched Jeremy busy himself about the banks of gauges and verniers.

Presently he came to the work station, sat down in front of a modern-looking terminal, and began typing quickly and dexterously.

"You know a lot about computers?"

"Hm? Uh, yeah, I guess. You?"

"Not much," Melanie said. "I use one, but mainly for word processing . . . Oh, sorry. You're busy."

"Nah, just doing some data entry. Be done in a sec."

Melanie watched him. He looked young, barely out of his teens. Was he out of his teens? She didn't know. He was reputed to be something of a wizard at computers. A "hacker." And she gathered, from what people had casually mentioned about Jeremy, that at one point he'd been in trouble for meddling in things he shouldn't have meddled in. But she knew nothing definite. At any rate, Jeremy was certainly a wizard in his own right, and held the post of Chief of Data Processing here in the castle.

Melanie swiveled her chair around and stared off into space, thinking.

She was brought out of her reverie by the sound of a door opening in the back of the lab. Two odd men came through. The tall one was Luster Gooch. Dolbert, very short and pot-bellied, was Luster's brother. Both wore tattered, grease-stained dungarees and equally shabby baseball caps. They came over to the work station.

Luster touched the bill of his cap. "Howdy, Miss Melanie."

Dolbert chittered, grinning bashfully.

"Hi, Luster. What have you guys been doing?"

"Oh, still tryin' to fix up that there space ship, or time machine, or whatever the heck ya call it."

"The *Sidewise Voyager*? I think it's an interdimensional spacetime ship. That's what everybody calls it."

"Wull, whachamacallit, we're still tryin' to fix the sucker. Every time someone brings it back from joy-ridin' it needs tinkerin' with agin."

"Any luck?"

"Oh, ah expect we'll get her workin' shortly."

"Great. Might come in handy with all this ruckus that's going on."

"All what ruckus, ma'am?"

Melanie was surprised. "You guys haven't noticed anything strange around the castle?"

Luster looked at Dolbert, who shrugged.

"Why no, ma'am," Luster said. "We been cooped up in the gravin' dock all day. Whut's goin' on?"

Just then the lab door burst open and a sword-wielding man in strange armor ran in. He was followed by another man in similar attire. The first man turned to meet the second's charge. Swords clashed.

Stunned, Melanie, Luster, and Dolbert watched. Jeremy kept typing.

Another pair of gladiators spilled into the room. There was much clanging about of steel.

"Should have locked that damn door," Jeremy muttered.

Two women came in. At least Melanie thought they were women. They were slightly smaller than the male gladiators, but well-muscled and very tough-looking. Both were wearing leather halters and briefs with steel greaves and brassards. They fought just as savagely as the men.

"Oh, my," Melanie said.

"Wull, don't that beat all," Luster said.

"Got it!"

Jeremy looked up from the terminal.

"What is it, Jeremy?"

"I've located the source of the disturbance. It's somewhere way down in the lower levels of the keep, near the King's Tower. It's probably in the cellar."

"Great. At least we know now. And when Incarnadine gets back . . ."

More combatants invaded the room, and the lab turned into a battleground.

"We'd better get the heck out of here," Jeremy said.

He, Melanie, Luster, and Dolbert all retreated through the back door. Jeremy slammed the door shut and turned the huge key in its lock, then pocketed it.

"That ought to hold 'em. We'd better get those—"

As he pointed to the room's other entrance, the two huge freight doors swung open and the gladiatorial melee spilled in.

"Into the *Voyager!*" Jeremy yelled.

The craft, sitting out in the middle of the spacious chamber, was bell-shaped, silvery, and rather small for four people, but it did accommodate a crew of that number. The nonhuman race that had built the craft were of considerably smaller dimensions.

Jeremy was the last one in. He wriggled through the tiny access hole and closed the circular hatch after him.

It was cramped inside.

"Excuse me, ma'am."

"Oh, that's all right."

"I think iffen you'd set right down here . . ."

"No, wait, let me get over here, then—"

Jeremy said, "Pardon me." Then he said, "Ouch, darn it."

Dolbert chortled.

"Dolbert's shore sorry he stepped on yore toe, there, Jeremy."

"Uh, that's okay. Just sit. Yeah, there."

All four settled into the uncomfortably small seats, the Gooch brothers in back, Jeremy and Melanie up front. The compartment was dim, the only light coming from glowing indicators on the instrument panel.

"Whew," Luster breathed.

"Yeah, really," Jeremy seconded.

"Well," Melanie said.

Jeremy slumped back. "Well, hell."

"Doesn't this thing have a window?" Melanie asked.

"Yeah, but it's polarized to opacity now. You want to see out?" Jeremy reached for a switch.

"No! They might see us."

"I can make it one-way."

"Forget it. I don't want to see what's going on out there." Melanie took a long, heaving breath. "What do we do now?"

"Good question," Jeremy said. "We're kinda stuck."

"We wait here till the ruckus is over, I guess," Melanie said with a shrug.

"When's that gonna be, though?"

"Jeremy, your guess is as good as mine."

"I'm not guessing."

"Should we make a run for it?"

It was Jeremy's turn to lift his shoulders. "We could get killed real easy, maybe."

Melanie nodded dolefully. "Maybe. But what other choices have we got? If we stay here . . ." She looked about the cramped compartment.

"No food, no water," Jeremy said. "No bathroom."

"Funny you should mention that," Melanie said, curling her lip.

Something thumped against the outside of the craft. Shouts and general commotion were heard.

"What are they doing?" Melanie wondered.

"Uh, they're, like, whacking on the ship."

"Why?"

"Rowdy bunch."

More whacks came against the craft's hull, resounding hollowly.

"Like being inside a garbage can when someone's beating it with a sledgehammer."

"Really," Jeremy agreed.

The *Voyager* shook with a heavy impact.

"Whoa!" Melanie looked worried. "What could they be doing now?"

"Maybe one of those elephants?" was Jeremy's surmise. "Want to look out?"

"No, forget it. We have to do something."

"Like?"

Melanie thought, then said, "Take the ship out."

"Out where?"

"Wherever it goes when it . . . you know, goes out."

"You mean out into the interdimensional thing?"

Melanie nodded emphatically. "What you said."

Looking at the control panel, Jeremy scratched his head. "Luster?"

"Yes, sir?"

"Is this ship in working order?"

"Don't know that."

"Why not?"

"Ain't tested her."

"Oh? I thought you—"

"Ain't had a chancet. We worked on fixin' 'er up all day, but ah cain't rightly say she's fixed up."

"Great." Jeremy flipped a few switches. Green lights lit up on the instrument panel. "She looks okay. All systems pretty much in 'Go' state."

Luster said, "Yup, I'd say."

The craft lurched again, this time more violently.

"I say we get the heck out of here now," Melanie voted.

Jeremy looked at her. Then he examined the control panel again. "Well, let's see if the motor turns over."

He threw a few more switches, pushed some buttons. The craft's engines came alive with a high-pitched whine.

"Yeah, it's running all right. Everything seems to check out." Jeremy turned his head to fix Melanie with a questioning stare, as if delegating the decision-making to her. "Do we take her out?"

Melanie blanched. "Jeez, I don't know. Is this thing safe? Does it work?"

"It usually does. Trouble is, every time I take it out I get into some kind of jam."

The tiny ship took another heavy assault from outside. It tipped and teetered. Loud clanging and banging commenced.

"We *are* in a jam," Melanie said.

"I guess so," Jeremy said. He reached and threw another switch.

The engine noise increased sharply in pitch, then subsided to a low, steady hum.

"Well, we're out," Jeremy announced.

"Where are we?"

"Oh, we're floating around in the non-space between the universes."

"Oh."

"Just kinda hanging out. You know."

"Uh, right. Just hanging out."

A red light blossomed on the instrument panel.

"Uh-oh."

Melanie swallowed hard. "What's that?"

"Navigation system."

"Navigation system?"

"Yeah. We don't have one now."

Melanie took a breath and held it. Then she let it out. "And that means . . . what?"

Jeremy settled back in the tiny pilot's seat.

He said: "It means we can't get back to the castle."

LIBRARY

THERE WAS CHAOS amidst the stacks.

Gladiators fought up and down the aisles, whooping
battle cries or letting out screams of agony: cases differed.
Swords clashed. Bookshelves toppled, sending fine first
editions, bound in skins of calf and lamb and kid, crashing
to the stone floor, there to be trampled underfoot. Huge
folios flew; quartos were drawn and quartered. Octavos lay
in tattered shreds.

The place was a shambles.

Osmirik the librarian sat in the midst of it all, sequestered
in his protected carrel, his long nose in a book; several, in
fact. He was a small man with a sharp face and soft eyes.
His expression was perennially sober and serious. He rarely
smiled. He favored the simple clothing of a scholar: a long
brown cloak with a hood.

As he pored over many a quaint and curious volume of
forgotten lore, part of his mind harked back to the many
times he had sought refuge in this little redoubt, a stone-
walled cubicle with a sliding door of stone that served well
as a barrier to the chaos without.

He redirected his attention to the task at hand: which was to discover what had gone awry in the castle. Somewhere within, a spell had gone amiss; that was obvious. The solution was to abrogate the spell—cancel it. The person who had cast the spell either could not cancel it or did not wish to do so. In either case it was up to another party to effect a solution to the problem; and in order to cancel someone else's spell, this other party first must know what kind of enchantment it was, what particular brand of magic was being practiced.

That was the immediate task. The table before him was heaped with grimoires, books of magical spells with instructions on how to cast them. He had eschewed the more obvious kinds of magic, bringing to the carrel only those books that smacked of the exotic, the off-beat, the heterodox.

He had not had much luck so far. Page after page bore his weary eye tràcks. It had been several hours since he'd started, but he had not hit on anything yet.

He closed one old leatherbound quarto, laid it aside, and chose another.

Well, what have we here? Ah, something called *A Book of Eldritch Charms and Divers Enchantments.* Not really so recondite, judging by the title. Open it up and let us see.

He read, flipped a page, read more. He riffled through the introductory sections to get to the meat.

There was no meat. Conventional magic with a few spices thrown in for savor. Nothing new. He'd bungled in choosing this one.

With a great sigh, he closed *Eldritch Charms* and laid hands on a little octavo, printed on cheap paper and bound in cloth, that was nothing more than a compendium of lists of books on magic, well-known and obscure. He paged through it.

What, exactly, was he looking for?

He sat back and folded his arms. Indeed. If only he could characterize the spell, describe its nature, he would then have a handle by which to grasp the problem.

Let's see: Dancing girls. Musicians. Entertainers. Definite thread there.

Janitorial homunculi. Hmmmm.

Gladiators.

Osmirik twiddled his thumbs. Gods, what could the connection be? Was there some pattern he was not seeing? Perhaps it was so obvious that he could not see it for its very simplicity.

Troubadours and gladiators. Well, the latter were considered entertainment in some cultures. But in others, religious ritual. What did troubadours and circus acts have in common? Or, for that matter, high-flown dance troupes and comedians? Surely the practice of a refined art form had nothing to do with animal acts or the telling of coarse jokes.

Marching bands. Oh, dear.

He flipped through the pages of the octavo. Grimoire after grimoire; but which one held the key?

Perhaps he would do better not to consider effects, but look to style. Was there some flavor to the spell that could provide a clue as to its origin? Osmirik considered the matter.

No, he could discern no identifiable signature. The magic surely was not Incarnadine's, or Trent's, nor did it evoke anyone whose style he might recognize. But the magic did have a flavor of sorts. It was . . . exotic, romantic. It struck him as self-indulgent, given to excess. Obviously it was a spell gone wild, out of control; but something told him that the spell was profligate in and of itself.

Could it be a pact with supernatural forces in which the

mortal signatory was granted any wish? In other words, had someone sold himself to demons? Perhaps. Or it was something similar. Not a pact, but the invocation of a malign spirit.

Perhaps it was a simple wish spell that had gone out of control. But it seemed too powerful to be simple. What about a very complex wish spell that involved the invoking of some powerful supernatural force, a malevolent one? What if that had got out of control?

What if . . . ? Ah, yes. Suppose an incompetent magician had got hold of a very dangerous grimoire, one that offered spells that only a past master could work without deleterious side-effects. Suppose further that this incautious neophyte botched the thing badly enough so as to give malign supernatural forces free rein to wreak havoc on an unsuspecting world.

Yes, suppose. It would be fruitful then to compile a list of exotic wish-granting spells.

But that would be a long list. Was there some way to narrow the list still further? Osmirik gave the possibility some thought.

Shouts and confusion outside. Someone or something crashed against the wall of the cubicle.

A spell botched this badly could only have come from a complete fool of a magician or one so naive as to dabble in dangerous magic without adequate preparation. Perhaps a very young or inexperienced magician; and it would help if that youngster was quite venal and not very bright. Such a one could stumble across . . .

He remembered something and sat up with a start. Had not a page come this morning bearing a message from Spellmaster Grosmond? Something about . . . Yes! The message said that a secret crypt had been discovered in the basement, and that this crypt was stuffed with some very

interesting articles, among which were several old books—
magical books, they appeared to be—which Osmirik, as
Royal Librarian, was supposed to examine to see if they
were of any value. Osmirik had read the message and made
a note on his calendar to go down there when, as Grosmond
suggested in his communication, the place had been swept
out a bit.

Osmirik rose from his seat. He must get to the basement
as soon as possible. But that presented a problem in itself.
Nevertheless, he was determined to attempt the passage, and
he had a possible means of assuring his safety.

He picked up yet another grimoire, a quarto volume in
lambskin embossed with gold. It, too, was a book of exotic
spells, among which was a spell of invisibility. With this
charm properly cast, Osmirik meant to pick his way through
the chaos. There were other enchantments he meant to use
as well, including a general facilitation spell. There was an
overriding problem with all this, however.

Osmirik was not a very good magician. In fact, he was
not much of a magician at all. He knew a great deal of
theory, but working efficacious magic was a matter of talent
as well as acumen. And talent, in the long run, was quite
possibly more important than acumen in the making of a
successful magician.

But now it was vitally important that he become a
successful magician, and in very short order.

He took his seat again, opened the book, and began to
study.

GRAND BALLROOM

WITH ONE MIGHTY SWEEP of his broadaxe, Snowclaw decapitated another opponent.

The head rolled across the parquetry and stopped, its bulging eyes staring up at the cut-crystal chandeliers. Then it disappeared, as did the headless body at Snowclaw's feet. Snowclaw didn't care for that. Better both should lie there and bleed satisfyingly for a while.

Nevertheless, Snowclaw was having one hell of a good time.

Another gladiator came at him, this one wielding a trident. Snowclaw swung the axe and clipped the weapon off at the prongs, then followed through, going into a graceful pirouette and bringing his blade whistling around again to take the man's legs off at the knees. Blood gushed, then vanished.

"Darn it."

Wasn't good sport just to disappear like that. The least they could do was hang around a minute and spill a little gore.

The room was clanging with gladiatorial action, but at the

moment no one else was free to engage Snowclaw. The great white beast waited impatiently.

"This is no fun."

He watched for a short time. None of these guys was any match for him. Or the females for that matter (and some of them were better than the males).

He left the ballroom and strode down the hall, swiping this way and that to clear a path. Soon everyone got the idea and stayed out of his way.

He met few challengers. At one point he witnessed a victory and was ready to do combat with the victor, but the latter took one look at the broadaxe and wanted no part of it.

"Aw, come on, fella."

"You're not even human!" was the man's excuse as he skedaddled.

"Lot of fun you are."

Snowclaw walked on. No one would give him so much as a glance. Growing frustrated, and even though it wasn't exactly fair, he whanged an unsuspecting combatant on the head as he passed, using the flat of the blade. The man was out for the count, of course, but aside from that . . .

He came to an elevator shaft—one of several in the keep—and pressed the DOWN button. Maybe another floor would provide more action.

He passed the time watching the proceedings. Then a soft chime sounded; the doors slid open and he stepped in. The only other passenger was a man strumming a battered guitar.

"Down?" Snowclaw asked.

The guitar player nodded. The man was lanky, red-haired, balding, rather homely, and wore scruffy clothes. He launched into a folk song.

Snowclaw did not know the tune (he knew no tunes, as

such), but instantly hated it. The man's voice was nasal and off-key (Snowy had perfect pitch) and just plain lousy. Nevertheless he belted out the lyrics, which were mawkishly sentimental and more than a little disingenuous in purport.

The elevator descended, and the man sang. Snowy was slightly embarrassed at first. Then he began to get irked.

Several minutes later the elevator was still plunging and the man had squeaked out half-a-dozen verses, all more or less the same. Even Snowclaw, who knew nothing about any kind of music, much less human music, could see that enough listening to this sort of drivel could lead to serious brain damage and an erosion of the finer sensibilities. It was repetitious, simplistic, hackneyed, and boring.

The man was singing right into Snowy's face. Snowy tried to ignore him, but the man persisted.

Snowy pushed him away, but the guy didn't get the idea. Snowy got all the more ticked off.

Still the elevator fell. Snowy stabbed desperately at the control panel.

Mercifully, the man finished. And segued neatly into another number, this one sounding like a plagiarism of the last; which in fact it was, though sung at even louder volume. Something about striking and forming a union.

With a growl. Snowy grabbed the guitar and smashed the thing over the folk singer's sparse-haired cranium.

The doors slid open. Snowy walked out. The doors closed again to hide from piteous view one scruffy prone figure wreathed in silent kindling.

Snowy didn't know how many floors he'd gone down, but it didn't really matter. This level was as replete with action and as scarce in respectable opponents.

A gladiator with a spear rushed at him.

Snowclaw sidestepped the shaft, warding it off neatly

with his free forearm. Then he pivoted and applied the flat of his blade sharply to the back of the attacker's head. The man went end over end, fetched up against the wall and lay still.

Snowy yawned, scratching his belly.

He moved on. Mingled among the fighters were more singers and dancers and such. These he ignored. Animals roamed the hallways. Some of them sniffed at Snowclaw in passing, but none seemed to be really interested. One or two growled, but that was all.

All was chaos, and the situation seemed to be getting worse with each passing minute. Snowclaw watched as a chorus line kicked past. Just what was this activity supposed to signify? He couldn't fathom it.

He stopped and looked around. A sunlit aspect lay to his right, at the far end of an alcove. A breeze came from it, and he relished the coolness. He was hot. Human habitations were usually uncomfortably warm for arctic beasts like Snowclaw. To him, frozen tundras were balmy.

Deciding to take a break, he crossed the alcove and strode through the aspect.

A pair of warring gladiators followed him through—and promptly vanished.

He came out into a grassy pasture bordered by trees. A pond lay to the right, lying placid at the bottom of a hollow. On a log at the rim sat Gene and Linda, eating a picnic lunch.

Gene turned, saw Snowclaw, and raised a hand.

"Hey!"

Snowclaw walked down to the pond.

"Hi, Snowy!" Linda said. "Where've you been?"

Snowclaw strode past them, threw the broadaxe on the grass, and dove into the pond with a mighty splash.

"Don't say hello," Gene said as he munched a kosher pickle.

"This stuff is getting a little wispy," Linda said, looking at her tuna salad sandwich.

"Not much taste." Gene watched the pickle in his hand disappear. "Not much to it, either."

"Rats. This aspect has lousy magic. But if I go back into the castle and whip up more food, it'll probably fizzle too when I bring it out."

"Not hungry anyway," Gene said.

Snowclaw's head broke the surface. He spat a needle-thin stream of water out between his great teeth.

"Hi, guys," he said. "I was hot."

"We gathered," Gene said. "You been noticing all the commotion inside?"

"Yeah. It was fun for a while. Then it got boring."

"We're trying to get to the bottom of it. Want to come along?"

"Sure. Got nothing better to do."

Snowclaw waded toward shore, pushing through tall marsh grass. When he climbed out, he wasn't as wet as one would expect. The water beaded on his thick white pelt and ran off easily. He helped the process with a few quick shakes.

Linda wiped water off her forehead. "Hey, take it easy, Fido."

"Sorry. Gosh, I'm hungry."

"I'd conjure something for you, but my magic doesn't seem to be working here."

"Don't bother. This stuff looks okay."

Snowclaw was referring to the tall grass at the pond's edge. He pulled up a clump and chewed the blades. He swallowed, then nodded.

"Not bad."

"Bet it goes better with a little pond scum," Gene suggested.

Snowclaw looked down. "Yeah? You mean that green stuff?"

"Snowy, don't!" Linda yelled, then scolded. "Gene, are you trying to make me sick again?"

"Just trying to be helpful."

"Behave yourself. Let's get back to business. What are we going to do when we get to the basement, if we can make it?"

Gene shrugged. "See what's what?"

"What do we do about the 'what'?"

"At least we can report to Incarnadine, tell him whatever the what is."

Linda nodded. "Okay, that sounds feasible. Because we're not going to be canceling this crazy spell, if that's what it is."

"You still think it's a spell gone bad?"

"Yeah, that's what it looks like. Somebody who didn't know what he was doing started something he couldn't finish."

"Or knew what he was doing and wanted to cause trouble."

"Well, he succeeded."

Gene threw a pebble into the pond. "I don't know, nothing's really happened so far. Actually, it's been kind of fun to watch."

"It won't be fun if the spell keeps going, which is exactly what it's going to do if somebody doesn't cancel it."

"What can happen?"

"The castle will become uninhabitable, that's what can happen."

"Oh. Anything else?"

"That's not enough?"

"I see what you mean."

Linda went on. "It'll become so clogged with crazy stuff that no one will ever be able to get in there and douse the spell. And if, as I suspect, this nutty thing is tapped into the castle's power, which is almost infinite . . . Get the picture?"

Gene watched a ripple reflect from shore and go outward again. "Hm. Never thought of that. All the worlds could be in danger."

"Now you're catching on."

" 'Chapter Twenty-one, In Which Our Heroes Once Again Save the Universe.' "

"You got it, keed."

"Funny thing is, where the hell is Incarnadine?"

Linda said, "You know, it's only been a few hours since the confusion started. He could have stepped out for something, intending to come right back."

"Right. If only the goofy stuff had begun just a tad earlier. He could have just snapped his fingers and tidied up the whole mess."

"God, I wish." Linda's shoulders fell. "I don't want to go down into any spooky basements."

"Do not be afraid, my dear," Gene said, doing a passable Bela Lugosi. "Those screams are merely the howling of the wind."

Linda frowned. "Gene, don't start with me. I hate spooky stuff, you know that."

"Why, I wasn't starting anything, my dear," he went on, now into his best Boris Karloff. "The basement is merely where I conduct my experiments in cell division and growth. What? You say you've never seen a spider that size? Why, the little devil must have gotten loose—"

Linda stared him down. "Gene," she said warningly.

"I'll stop. Thing is, I don't think we'll make it."

"To the basement? Why not?"

"The congestion is increasing geometrically the farther down we go."

Linda nodded glumly. "Yeah. Well, we have to try."

"We'll need your magic in there."

"No problem. I can create a shield."

"The old magical force screen."

"But it'll make maneuvering harder."

"Always some dues to pay for magic," Gene said.

"True. Well, shall we give it a go?"

"Once more into the dumpster, dear friends." Gene got up. "Let's get moving."

Snowclaw had pulled up a major portion of the grass at the edge of the pond.

"Not much to this stuff," he commented, "but it is tasty. Specially the little dab of mud that comes up from the bottom."

Linda's face soured. "Snowy, you're making me ill."

"Sorry. I'm hungry."

"Snowy, you're *always* hungry."

"'The sedge has withered from the lake,'" Gene said. "'And no birds sing.'"

"Where?" Snowclaw said, looking around eagerly.

"You leave those poor birds alone, Snowy," Linda reprimanded. "We're going now."

"I'm going to be starving in a little while."

"I'll whip up something for you in the castle," Linda assured him. "Come along, Snowclaw."

"Yes, ma'am."

Linda started walking up the hill.

When she'd gotten halfway up, Snowclaw asked, "Are most human females as bossy as Linda is sometimes?"

Gene put a finger to his lips. "Shhh. You are treading

very dangerous ground, my friend. Not PC, if you get my drift.''

"Huh?''

'' 'Into the valley of death rode the six hundred,' and all that.''

"What?''

"Let's go.''

"Oh. All right.''

Scratching his massive white head, Snowclaw followed Gene up the hill.

ARENA

THE ARENA SHOOK with the roar of the crowd. Howls of blood lust resounded. The crowd was average for a Saturday night.

On the sandy floor at the base of the vast circus, several contests were going on. One, not properly a contest, involved lions attacking helpless victims. Another featured a clash of cavalries, horses neighing and rearing amidst the rising dust of battle. Still another pitted charioteers against spear-carrying men on foot. The former were winning.

Thorsby regained consciousness and sat up. He looked out across the arena, then swung his feet over the edge of his divan.

He tried to get up. He couldn't quite make it and sat back down heavily.

"Is something wrong, great Caesar?"

"Eh? Uh, no. I've had enough. I'm heading up."

"Why, O Magnificent One?"

"I've a bleedin' headache. And besides that, I've seen everything."

"A thousand pardons if I contradict the divine Caesar, but you have seen nothing yet!"

Thorsby looked bleary-eyed at the houri who had entreated him. "Oh? I'd like to know what else there is. I've gobbled all the grub, guzzled all the grog, did all the naughty bits. Wonderful, wonderful, but, really . . ."

"What is it, Divine One?"

"Well, you know . . ." Thorsby chuckled. "It's all a spell, really. Just a conjuration. Means nothing, all hocus pocus, don't you know. It was all a bit of fun, but we really have to be getting back to work. Matter of fact, I do think we're in serious trouble already. Where the blazes is Fetchen? Fetchen!"

"Methinks, Divine One, thou knowest not the true trouble thou'rt in."

Thorsby got unsteadily to his feet. "Fetchen, old boy? Now, where did that rascal get to—"

Thorsby's face collided with a massive naked chest. He stepped back and looked up. The owner of the chest was an immense figure in a turban, voluminous pants, and long pointed slippers. The man (if that is what he was) stood with his sinewy arms folded, one hand grasping the haft of an immense scimitar, its wicked curving blade upraised and gleaming.

"Going somewhere?" the man asked pointedly.

Thorsby took another step back. "Uh, well, yes. More or less. Time to cancel the spell."

"Cancel the spell?" The huge man shook his head. "I'm afraid not."

"Oh?" Thorsby's voiced squeaked. He cleared his throat. "Why not?"

"We get this chance very seldom. We shall not miss it."

"Chance for what, exactly?"

"To come out into the world. To be alive. Very tiresome simply to exist as potential, with no actuality."

"Oh. Yes, well, I'm afraid that can't be helped, old boy.

You'll have to go back into your bottle or lamp or whatever. The whole lot of you, in fact. It was a bit of fun, but—''

''That will not happen, great one.''

Thorsby made an effort to gather himself together. ''See here. You're forgetting who the magician is, who's in charge of this whole charade.''

''That is not forgotten, master. But these obligations are not one-sided. By giving us unlimited license, you have opened a door that is not easily shut.''

Thorsby nodded. ''I see, I see.'' He looked around. ''Well, we'll just have a look at that grimoire. Around here someplace . . .'' Thorsby got down on his knees and searched.

''You won't find it, master.''

''Eh? I won't?''

''No.''

''Oh. Well.'' Thorsby rose and dusted off his hands. ''Then we'll throw a general cancellation spell on the whole affair and see what happens.''

The turbaned man ran a thick finger delicately along the blade of his scimitar. ''Master would not want to do that.''

''And why not?''

''Because master would not get the second word out of his mouth if he uttered the first.''

The turbaned man grasped the curving sword in both meaty hands and swished it about viciously.

''Does my master understand the full import of my words?''

Thorsby took a deep breath and let it out slowly. ''Yes. Quite.''

The turbaned apparition smiled. ''Meanwhile, your every wish will be indulged. Does my master wish anything?''

''A drink.''

The man held out his hand. A goblet full of purple liquid

appeared on his palm. He extended his arm toward Thorsby.

"A drink for my master."

Thorsby took the goblet and drank. His eyes widened.

"Why, this is super. Super! I've never tasted wine like this. It's . . . well, I can't believe it, but it's better than the other stuff!"

"Only a foretaste of what is yet to come. I bid thee, sit, O divine Caesar. Disport thyself!"

"Enough of the Caesar bit, please. Let's go back to sultan, or caliph, or shah, or something. All this spilling of guts is making me queasy."

"Your slightest whim is graven in stone, great and wonderful master!"

Thorsby lay back down on the divan. He drank, and marveled again at the taste of wine.

Then his face lapsed into a worried frown.

"Grosmond is going to be ever so pissed off at us," he said to himself.

WAR ZONE

KWIP FLATTENED HIMSELF against the turf as more artillery shells fell in the vicinity of the clearing, not far away. He had been under fire once or twice before, but had never experienced the terror of these weapons. The explosions pierced his ears like crossbow bolts and the concussion was almost enough to knock him senseless.

Nevertheless he clung to consciousness until all was quiet once again.

When he thought it safe, he rose slowly. Now, to find the portal.

He was sure the magic doorway was very near. As best he could surmise, it lay directly across the clearing from where he had crouched in the underbrush, hiding from the lion—the lion which had never materialized. He had been walking straight back across the clearing when the bombardment started.

But the portal was nowhere in sight.

Was it possible that he could have got turned about widdershins? In that case, the portal would be directly across from where he was right now. But he could not be sure. No telling which way he had run.

The clearing was slightly oval, its border lacking distinguishable features. The shelling had put him in a dither; he was now completely disoriented. Perhaps if he crossed again—but he feared renewed shelling. He resolved, therefore, to keep to the wood, which offered some protection against the blasts.

Kwip drew his sword.

He made his way through the underbrush, keeping as close as possible to the edge of the clearing, yet still leaving a margin of safety. He ducked under low branches, pushed through tangles of vines and weeds. It seemed to be late spring here. The smell of wildflowers was in his nostrils, though he couldn't see any, not at the moment.

He tripped over an exposed root and stifled a curse. All was quiet; not even the birds had recovered their composure. No insects buzzed. He stopped, squatted, and peered out into the clearing. Lumps of raw, red clay had been thrown up by the explosions out of deep craters. He'd have to watch himself when and if he crossed again.

He moved on. At length he stopped again, now totally befuddled. Where was that confounded portal?

There came to his ears a strange whirring sound, and he could not for the life of him imagine what could be making it. He thought of a great metallic bird.

He was astonished when such a creature landed in the clearing. Well, "creature" it may have been, in a manner of speaking; it flew and had stubby wings and spindly legs or supports. It was made of some sort of metal, though a metal painted in stripes of brown and green. Yes, a strange thing to behold; but he was well aware that it was an infernal machine of some sort. It looked wickedly destructive, bristling with rods and other projections—armaments of some kind, he guessed.

The thing settled into the clearing, the *shush-shush* of its whirling blades strangely quiet. Its engines whined softly. Kwip had seen depictions of similar craft in books in the castle library. This specimen looked to be of a higher species. It was bulbous in parts, yet sleek and supple elsewhere. It had short wings, and the engines appeared capable of rotating from vertical to horizontal. He had never seen this particular craft depicted, but had seen its progenitors.

A hatch on the craft's side opened and metal men spilled out. Soldiers.

Kwip was astonished again. Were these human beings or mechanical men? They were completely encased in metal—dappled, like the craft, in a strange mix of brown and green hues—from helmet to shoes. Yet they did not clank and lurch about; they moved as men, with but a faint hissing noise accompanying their movements. Six of them fanned out from the craft to take up defensive positions in a circle about it. They swung their weapons back and forth warily, on guard. Kwip could only imagine the coldly efficient eyes which lay hidden behind the dark glass that fronted their helmets. If indeed they had eyes at all.

The defensive circle widened, each soldier advancing radially. One was coming directly at Kwip, who now felt himself on the prickly horns of a dilemma. If he retreated, it would be into unknown territory, one torn by war. If he moved toward the clearing and the portal, he would be discovered and possibly shot.

He gave thought to retreating a safe distance and waiting for the invading troop to reboard the craft and fly away. But there was risk in that course of action as well. What if this lot were engaged in reconnoitering? They might be scouting the area in search of a suitable site for a camp.

Unsettling thought, that. He'd never gain access to the portal. He would be stranded here, possibly forever.

No. Only one thing to do. Make a mad dash for it across the clearing, cutting cater-corner. They would no doubt fire at him, but Kwip prided himself on his fleetness of foot. He would at least have a sporting chance, he thought.

Suddenly, on the far side of the clearing, a sizzling bolt of fire erupted from one of the soldiers, emanating from the barrel of his arquebus, or whatever it was. The bolt hit the trees, sending flames skyward.

Kwip gulped. Perhaps he would not have a sporting chance after all.

Nevertheless, he was determined to make the attempt.

But in what direction should he run? What was his destination to be? He scanned the circuit of the clearing, to no avail. He could detect neither hide nor hair of the portal, that elusive doorway back to the castle and relative safety (if a lion did not devour him immediately upon his arrival!).

The soldier nearest him was still advancing, and the time was at hand for a decision. Kwip thought hard and furiously.

No, he'd have to retreat. If the portal had not vanished, it was probably directly behind the strange craft. In that case a mad dash would be foolish. Truth be told, without knowledge of the portal's exact whereabouts, a mad dash would be silly in any case.

He turned to beat a retreat and found himself on a narrow path, little more than a rabbit trail, that led away from the clearing. Creeping along on all fours, he followed it.

A voice—amplified by some means—barked behind him. Suddenly the heat of fire seared his back.

They were shooting at him! The trees bordering the clearing were in flames.

He got up and ran, wondering how he had been seen. But who knew with what wizardry these demons augmented their inhuman senses?

Out of the corner of his eye he caught sight of a stone corridor. He skidded to a stop.

The portal! It had been here, behind him, all the while. At that moment he remembered running a short distance through woods before coming out into the clearing. Scatterbrained fool!

He sprinted back along the rabbit trail. As he did, he saw the soldier enter the woods and take aim at him. He made a wild dive for the opening.

He tumbled through the portal and back into the castle, ending up on his back on the flagstones. He jumped to his feet and ran to the nearest intersecting hallway and hid behind the corner.

He peeked out.

The soldier was framed in the portal, seeming to peer within, weapon at the ready. Then he walked off, only to appear again and shake his head. There was confusion in his manner. Apparently, to Kwip's great relief, the soldier—or this diabolical machine that took a soldier's form—could not perceive the portal.

Kwip was safe.

Something poked him in the back and he jumped and whirled about, sword raised and ready to strike.

"Put that thing down, you crazy fool!"

It was the woman of color, Deena Williams, and her sometime paramour, Barnaby Walsh. Kwip exhaled and sheathed his sword.

"Jumpy, ain't he?" Deena asked of Barnaby.

"You ought not surprise a man like that," Kwip warned.

"Some trouble up ahead?" Barnaby asked.

Kwip looked toward the portal. The soldier walked by

again, still oblivious to the phenomenon in front of him: a doorway to another world.

Kwip shook his head. "None now, but you don't want to go through that aspect."

"We been duckin' in and out of aspects for the last couple hours," Deena told him. "Hidin' from all this garbage goin' on."

Kwip nodded. "Which I've been doing as well." He suddenly remembered his abandoned booty and looked wildly about.

Over Barnaby's shoulder he saw the glint of gold. He ran for it.

It was a gold drinking cup; as he picked it up he caught sight of a necklace lying on the stone not far way.

The stuff was scattered all over, kicked by dancers, nuzzled by lions, punted about by marching feet. Gods knew how wide an area it had been strewn over, all lying there, waiting for anyone to pick up.

Kwip began searching, dashing around frantically, scooping things up, hurrying to the next item. Another necklace, a sapphire ring . . . a chalice . . . a bracelet . . .

"Uh, is all this stuff yours?" Deena asked.

"Yes," Kwip said over his shoulder.

The sound of a brass band grew near, and Kwip cursed. The commotion was returning in force after what must have been a momentary lull.

"You ought to stick with us," Barnaby said. "We're going to find a nice aspect to hide out in."

"I must recover my valuables!" Kwip shouted as he ran to recover a diamond pendant. He was amazed that anything was left.

"You're nuts!" Deena yelled. "Let's get out of here," she said to Barnaby.

"Right," Barnaby said. Then he shouted at Kwip again. "You're absolutely sure?"

"Off with you!" Kwip shouted back. "I'll be all right!"

"Okay, good luck!"

The pair left Kwip to his valuables and his foolish greed.

Presently, two very large cats came prowling around the corner, a whiff of fresh meat in their bewhiskered nostrils.

PLAIN

HIS TENT HAD A GOOD VIEW of the citadel. The fortress of Troas, well-built and lovely, its beetling walls formidably high, bestrode a hill overlooking the plain. On the north circuit, topless towers soared above the highest rampart. From the walls, from the towers, had come a lethal rain of arrows, spears, rocks, and boiling oil, with sacks of excrement thrown in for comic relief. It seemed the Dardanians had an endless supply of war materiel and that no siege, however long, would exhaust their stores.

For two long years now, the Arkadian armies had tried to breach those angled walls, to scale them, to undermine them. Frustrated eyes had long beheld those towers, and tired, defeated minds had imagined them ablaze, destroyed for all time, their rain of death ended.

But not yet. The siege went on endlessly, and so did the single-combat contests. Dauntless heroes from each side had locked in mortal combat, one on one. Victories had gone to both sides. In this respect the score was about even. But Dardanians were winning the siege, wearing down the Arkadian attackers. Arkadian supplies were low. There were only so many coastal towns to raid for food and other necessities.

It was not a true siege, because the Dardanian army still had access to the sea. Troas was still linked to supply lines, though those were growing more tenuous. The Arkadians had ceaselessly harassed supply ships, to some effect.

Two long years. Two agonizingly long years.

Trent lay on his recliner, drinking plundered Dardanian wine. He was not quite drunk but was getting there. He had given up hope of getting back to the castle and Sheila. He was stranded. There had been no communication from Inky, no message of any sort. Trent felt abandoned and alone.

And defeated. His strategies and tactics had for the most part not worked against the Dardanians. They were stronger than anyone had imagined, and devilishly resourceful to boot. Outnumbered, they had fought the Arkadians to a standstill. The towers of Troas still stood.

With some effort, he got up and went to the tent's entrance, held back a flap, and looked out. Nothing was happening on the front today. A fight had broken out in the camp of the Arkadians. Some squabble about who should inherit a dead trooper's armor. The sky was clear above the citadel, a few fast clouds scudding by. He looked to his left and gazed at the distant rocky heights of Mount Eta for a long moment, then brought his eyes back to the camp. Someone had just run someone through with a spear. A major brawl was breaking out.

The constant bickering disgusted Trent. He closed the flap, returned to his recliner and his wineskin.

He was at the end of his tether. Somehow he had to bring this farce to some sort of conclusion, get back to Arkadia and slip back through the portal (not far from Mykos), and hope the time-compression effect had been enough to render his two-year subjective absence into something objectively tolerable—say, a few months. Even at that, Sheila still might brain him with a potted palm.

If only he could bring himself to go back on his pledge not to work large-scale magic!

Such as, say, conjuring a small tactical nuke . . .

No. For any number of reasons—not the least of which was the problem of differing physical laws in different universes—that would not do at all. But what else? Fire spells, zone-of-death spells . . . Actually those were more defensive than offensive. Did he know exactly how to go about constructing siege engines? No, not really; not without a little research. How about whipping up a couple of flintlocks? Too many technologies involved.

Hexes. He could brew up something that would have the Dardanians dropping like flies. Mysterious plagues. Biological warfare!

Damn, that wouldn't do either. He had never been very good at working those kinds of spells. Besides, as amoral as he liked to think he was, there were certain ethical considerations that he couldn't quite get around.

Moreover, he had been charged with a purely military task. Inky's instructions allowed him to employ only those supernatural aids which were divinatory or clairvoyant in nature. Intelligence-gathering. In that, he had been successful. Knowing the exact positions of enemy forces had enabled the Arkadians to take and hold these strategically important flood-plains, sodden and swampy though they were.

Which left most of the high ground to the enemy, true. But they were already up there.

He took another swig of sweet Dardanian wine. Good stuff, if a little heavy. Got you drunk anyway, and that was all that counted.

Tactical magic was out. He'd already tried to sneak in

some strategic ploys, since the big show on the high altar. In fact, he'd tried the lightning-summoning bit again, bringing a fierce thunderstorm down on Troas. Lightning strikes had started a good number of fires. But the upshot was that Troas still stood. The fires had been a major nuisance, but nothing more.

And afterward, he'd lain semicomatose for almost a week. The spell had taken a lot out of him.

On the non-supernatural front, the undermining had been his idea, and this gambit had shown great possibilities until the Troadeans had copped to what was going on and had flooded the mine, using water from their hot springs. Two hundred men had lost their lives in that debacle.

Remembering, Trent shuddered. Being parboiled alive like that, like a lobster. Ugh.

And he could have easily been caught in there himself. A miracle he hadn't. What would Sheila have—?

He chuckled. He must really love that woman. Yes, he did. He *must* get back to her. Her red hair was so lovely, her skin so fair, freckled here and there. Breasts large and full for such a slim woman . . .

"Trent?"

"Huh?"

Telamon was standing in front of him.

"Must have dozed off . . ."

"Sorry to wake you."

Trent sat up, feeling tired and logy. "Think nothing of it. Something up?"

"Not really. But I wanted you to know that I talked the king out of arresting you again."

Trent chuckled. "Kind of you. Why did you do it? Some wine?"

"No, thank you."

"Uh, pull up something and sit."

"Thank you very much."

Telamon piled some sheepskins together and sat cross-legged.

He said, "Why did I do it? Because I rather admire you. Like you, even."

"Same here." Trent took a swig of wine. "What was eating Anthaemion this time?"

"Nothing especially. He wants scapegoats and thinks your beard the longest."

Trent looked around. "You'd best guard your tongue, my friend."

"There is no one about, and you will not repeat my words."

"No, I won't. Go on."

Telamon shrugged. "There is no more. Eventually he will have you killed, or kill you himself. But he is afraid of you. You are a sorcerer. He keeps repeating rumors about you."

"Rumors? What rumors?"

"Those that circulate among the troops. One of them has it that you change yourself into an animal at night and prowl. One story says that you change yourself into a great bat and devour people."

Trent laughed. "I don't have the right accent."

"Can you do it?" Telamon asked.

"Do what?"

"Change yourself into an animal."

Trent snorted. "Any sorcerer worth his salt can do an animal tranformation. Not that I do that traditional stuff much. When I was a kid I once changed myself into an eagle. I soared. Soared. Kind of liked that." Trent was silent a moment, staring off, remembering. Then he looked at his visitor. "Anthaemion still expects me to win this war for him, doesn't he?"

"Yes, I am afraid so."

"Well, I can't."

"He thinks you are in fact against him."

"Yeah, he would think that."

"Are you?"

Trent smiled. "Are you sure you won't repeat *my* words?"

Telamon was disappointed. "I had numbered myself among your confidants. It seems I was presuming."

"Not at all. You want to know my opinion of Anthaemion? He's a major asshole."

Telamon could not suppress a smile.

"And I'll give you another opinion. I'm sick of this pack of morons you call an army. Thugs, every one of them. Pirates. I've seen biker gangs with more redeeming virtues."

"I'm sorry—?"

"Swaggering bullies. And as to their military prowess, none of them knows the first thing about discipline, about following orders. They are little better than a rabble, no matter how they strut and brag." Trent snorted. "Heroes. These jerks wouldn't know heroism if it came up and bit 'em on the backside."

Telamon brooded a moment before admitting, "I am afraid there is something in what you say."

"You bet your ass. Sorry, I'm not blaming you or including you in my sweeping generalizations. You're a man of some breeding and you have a head on your shoulders."

Telamon bent his head. "My humble thanks."

"But the rest . . ." Trent shook his head. He reached, rummaged among some debris, and finally came up with a wooden cup. He poured wine into it and let the skin drop. He drank.

"But we cannot stay here forever," Telamon said.

"I'd quit the whole business if I could," Trent said. "But, although I'm a potential deserter, I'm no traitor. When I sign on with an outfit, my loyalty is part of the bargain."

"I have assured the king of that very fact."

"It's true. I also gave my word to my brother. My word, the word of a prince, counts for something, you know. I take that stuff seriously."

Telamon's face registered momentary shock. Then he quickly rose and bowed solemnly.

Puzzled, Trent asked, "What's up?"

"I ask your forgiveness for sitting in your presence. I was not aware—"

"Oh, that. Sit down, pal. Here, I'm a courtier, and one out of favor. In my world, it's different."

"In your—? I do not understand."

"Sit down, please."

Reluctantly, Telamon reseated himself.

Trent went on. "It's hard to explain, but we—my brother and I—are from a place so far away that it's hard not to call it a different world altogether. Unimaginably far away."

"I see."

"In fact, it's . . . Forget it, we'll leave it at that."

"Your magic must be godlike."

"Well, shit." Trent took another swallow of wine. "It can be. If I put my mind to it I could . . . Ahhh, fuck the whole business."

"Sweet wine can make one bitter," Telamon said.

"I'm not bitter, I'm ticked off. At my brother, mainly. For stranding me here."

"One can imagine."

"So, it's up to me to find a way out of this mess." Trent

poured himself more fortitude, sampled it. Then he looked at Telamon. "Have any ideas?"

"The glimmerings of one."

"Spill it. I'm fresh out of glimmerings."

Telamon brooded at some length, then said, "If we could employ stealth instead of brute force, perhaps . . ."

"Out with it. I'm all for stealth at this point."

"I had a dream the other night. I dreamt of a great horse—"

Trent looked pained. "Oh, no."

Telamon frowned.

Trent said, "Does this idea of yours have something to do with hiding some guys inside a big wooden horse?"

Telamon was astounded. Awed as well, he shook his head. "Is there no hiding even dreams from a sorcerer?"

Trent grinned. "Sorry, it's not that I'm peeking into your noggin, it's just—never mind. No, the horse thing is silly. Forgive me, but do you really think the Troadeans are dumb enough to fall for something like that? They'd build a fire under the thing first to see if anyone yelped. I'd drill a few holes and run a spear or two through. First thing I'd think of, once I saw that the enemy had pulled up stakes and vamoosed, leaving this huge fucking statue of a horse. Wouldn't you?"

Telamon laughed. He nodded. "I suppose I would."

"Oh, there's a chance, I suppose." Trent drank again. "No, I take that back. That scheme has about as much chance as a fart in a—"

Something seemed to occur to Trent just then. He stared off into space.

Telamon studied his face. After a longish while he said, "You have an idea."

Presently, Trent's attention returned to the here-and-now.

He spilled the rest of the wine into the dirt, then tossed the cup into a corner.

He smiled. ''I do. As they say right before the fadeout, 'Now, here's my plan . . .' ''

HIGH IN THE AIR

DYING WASN'T SO BAD, once you got over the initial panic.

This thought came to Dalton as he fell. At first there had been a numbing terror. Then . . . nothing. He'd blacked out.

Now? Peace. Great peace. His life was over. It had been a good life, all told. Not that there weren't a few things he regretted. Difficult to avoid all the rough spots. But overall, he'd enjoyed living. And he was grateful for the castle. Yes, especially for the castle. The privilege of living in Perilous for just a few years had been enough to make it all worthwhile.

Marvelous place, even though it killed him in the end.

Another thought came to him: he'd been falling for an awfully long time. A bit too long, really. Maybe he was already dead.

He opened his eyes. Sky above. He rolled his head. There was the ground, and he was surely heading toward it. But there was something wrong. His sense of time was distorted.

Was it true, the old saw about your entire life flashing in front of your eyes? Well, he was indeed feeling a bit retrospective. Maybe when you die this compressed time thing happens, and it takes forever to actually kick the old bucket. Good thing dying wasn't all that unpleasant.

He was falling. He could feel and hear the air rush past. But he wasn't falling very fast. What was the formula? Feet per second squared times the gravitational constant g . . . something like that. He should be plummeting, really dropping. But he wasn't. This was rather peculiar.

He craned his neck to look at the ground again. Yup. Still getting closer, but not as fast as the last time he'd looked.

This was *damned* peculiar. Was he going to die or wasn't he? Here he had gotten used to the idea, had even arrived at the point where he was thinking, well, maybe it isn't such a bad thing after all; in fact, maybe it's the old proverbial consummation devoutly to be wished—and now it seemed there was some doubt about the whole business. Hmph. Well, that didn't wash with him. If you fall off a high parapet, you're damned well supposed to die, and that's all there is to it.

Slowly, he tumbled over until he was dropping face forward, like a skydiver in free fall.

Except that he was doing blessed little diving. This was more like floating, for pete's sake. Floating? What the blue blazes was going on here?

Out of the air, a familiar voice came to him.

Hello, there! This is your lucky day. You've managed to trip one of the castle's safety spells. This one is designed to catch people who have been heroic, clumsy, or just plain dumb enough to fall out of a window or off a battlement. Only you know which case applies! Whichever it is, though, you're quite safe. The levitation spell will lower you safely to the ground. No need to worry. If you've been heroic, you have my thanks. If not . . . do try to be more careful in the future. Have a nice day.

The voice was Incarnadine's.

"Well, I'll be damned," Dalton said.

After a superhuman effort, Thaxton managed to pull himself up.

He spilled over onto the walkway and lay on his back, not really caring that lions might devour him at any moment. He felt sick with grief, wanting to die himself. He almost would have preferred to fall than watch Dalton do it.

The funny business above the castle was still going on, though he couldn't quite make out the strange smirking face. Bright things flapped in the air above the parapets, among rainbows of unnatural color.

Presently, he thought he might get up. He raised himself to a sitting position and looked about him.

No lions.

Well. He got to his feet, an act that took slightly more strength than he seemed to possess. He went to the parapet and looked over the edge.

It was a frightfully long way down. He couldn't see a thing, and he didn't really want to. There was no chance that Dalton had survived, and he had no need to see evidence confirming the fact.

He'd best get back downstairs. It would devolve to him to apprise everybody of the grim event.

Nasty business. Nasty, nasty business.

He headed back to the tower.

Like Buck Rogers with his antigravity belt (he still remembered those old serials!), Dalton settled gently to earth, feet first.

He felt a little wobbly, but otherwise fine. He stood in the middle of a high-walled courtyard. An arched gateway lay to his right, and he walked to it.

He entered another courtyard. He crossed it, going through another gate.

After traversing a maze of cloisters, courtyards, and barbicans, he finally found what he thought was the exterior wall of the keep. He kept it to his right as he continued to thread his way through the labyrinth.

Finally, he saw a pair of mammoth bronze doors. No knobs or door handles, but strangely enough there was, set into the stone wall beside one door, a button that looked like a doorbell. He pressed it. A deep chime sounded inside.

After a longish moment, he pressed it again. As he was about to do it a third time, a small wicket opened in the right-hand door and a strange-looking Guardsman poked his head out.

"Who is it?"

"Uh, my name's Dalton, and I—"

The Guardsman, who looked like some cartoon character, was annoyed. "Can't you read the sign?"

"I fell off the, uh . . . What? Oh. That."

Only then did Dalton notice the neatly hand-painted sign on the wall to his right. In archaic script, it read:

DOORBELL OUT OF ORDER—PLEASE KNOCK

"Interesting."

The Guardsman's head withdrew and the tiny door closed.

Dalton knocked. The sound echoed inside.

After a while he knocked again. Just to be sure, he pressed the bell button a few more times.

Finally, there came clanking sounds from inside. The door opened a crack.

Another Guardsman, this one looking quite normal and

not like something out of an old movie, peered out and registered recognition. "Mr . . . Dalton, is it?"

Dalton said, "Yes. This is rather embarrassing, but I fell off the roof of the castle."

"Ye gods! Are you all right, sir?"

"Fine. The safety spell saved me."

"Thank the heavens! Come in, sir, come in."

The Guardsman admitted him.

Inside, Dalton looked up at the other side of the immense door. He could see no wicket nor even the suggestion of one.

"Very interesting."

"Sir?"

Dalton grinned at the gatekeeper. "Nothing." He chuckled. "Never a dull moment in this place, is there? Not even a slightly dull moment."

The Guardsman shook his head sadly. "I'm afraid not, sir. I'm afraid not."

BETWEEN THE UNIVERSES

"WELL," MELANIE SAID, "where do we go from here?"

The interior of the *Voyager* was dark except for myriad tiny lights, many of them glowing a panicky red, on the instrument panel. The temperature had been pleasant at first, but now was rising into the uncomfortable range.

Luster and Dolbert were phlegmatically silent in the back seat. Nothing ever seemed to unsettle them.

"Actually, there's no direction in non-space," Jeremy said.

"What the heck is 'non-space,' anyway?"

"I dunno if I can explain. It's sort of like, well, actually it's an extra dimension over and above the four dimensions of normal space. Something like that. Only it's just one dimension. We're really not in it, just riding on it like on a sheet of ice. As long as we keep moving, which we are, we stay on that plane. If we slow down or stop, we drop through into normal space."

"Oh. But you said we can't get back to the castle."

"Right. Without the navigation system, the ship doesn't know what direction the castle's in. Get the picture?"

"I think. What can we do?"

"Well, first we have to get out of non-space, 'cause non-space isn't such a great place to be for too long. So, we gotta drop back in somewhere."

"You mean drop back into real space? Like, where?"

"Well, that's just the thing. We aren't gonna know where until we drop in. It'll be some universe. I just hope it's not one of the weird types."

Melanie knew all about the weird types. She'd been stranded in one of them once. It was enough for her.

Jeremy was chewing his bottom lip.

"What's the matter?" she asked.

"I was just wondering if I should boot up Isis."

"Isis?"

"You never met Isis. She's a program."

Melanie was confused. "A program?"

"Yeah. Actually, a cross between a spell and a utility program. She's an artificial intelligence, and, I guess, a spirit of some kind."

"What kind of spirit?"

"I really don't know. It bothers me sometimes to think about it. But she's also a program, and I got her loaded into the ship's computer."

"I see," Melanie said. After being reminded, she remembered hearing of Isis. Some spirit! A knockout brunette who was totally devoted to Jeremy and who made the female-shy Jeremy more than a little nervous.

"She always helps, but sometimes she gets a little bossy."

Melanie was about to reply, when a voice came out of a speaker on the instrument panel.

Jeremy, that hurt!

Jeremy's face flushed. "Damn it, I forgot that I have her programmed to automatically boot up with engine start. Sorry, Isis."

The voice said, *Well, you should be.*

"I didn't mean it, honest. I appreciate your help. It's just that when someone makes a lot of suggestions I get kind of confused. Sometimes I'm better off just working on a problem myself."

I understand, honey. Really, I don't want you to feel that I'm here to boss you around. You're the user, darling, not me. I'm just a utility program.

"Heck, you're more than that. You're a person."

Thanks, baby. But I'm not much of one when I don't have my virtual body.

Melanie thought, *And I've heard it's one helluva great virtual body.*

Jeremy said, "It's kinda cramped in here at the moment."

Oh, I don't take up so much space. Please?

"Uh . . . okay. Sure. Just watch where you materialize."

Melanie wondered where in the cramped compartment someone could possibly "materialize" without landing on top of someone else.

Isis suddenly appeared, sitting in Jeremy's lap, her knees jutting sharply up over Melanie's. She wore a short black cocktail dress that exposed most of her long shapely legs. She was dark-haired, blue-eyed, and simply beautiful.

"Hi, honey!" She kissed Jeremy on the lips.

Jeremy blushed. "Hi, Isis. Nice to see you again. Uh, Isis, this is Melanie."

Isis smiled warmly at Melanie. "Hello, Melanie."

"And you know the Gooches."

"Hello, boys. Nice to see you again."

The Gooch brothers tipped their moth-nibbled baseball caps.

Luster beamed, "Pleasure's all ours, Miss Isis."

Dolbert cooed, bashfully averting his eyes.

"Now," Isis said. "We have a problem, don't we?"

"Yup," Jeremy said. "We sure do. Do you think it's hardware or software?"

"That's a toughie. We're going to have to figure that out first. If it's hardware, we may have to land somewhere to make repairs."

"That's always risky," Jeremy said.

"True, but we might not have any choice. Drop the ship into normal space, Jeremy."

"If I can reach."

"Just put your arms around here, baby. I'm not ticklish."

Melanie thought, *This woman, or whatever she is, really knows how to handle men. Maybe she can teach me a few tricks.*

"Okay," Jeremy said, "I have it."

Isis giggled. "Do you really know what you have in your hand?"

"Ooops! Sorry."

Isis laughed as Jeremy's face got beet-red.

Oh, brother! Melanie thought.

"Okay, we're through, or out . . . or whatever."

"Would you like me to clear the view port, Jeremy dear?"

"Check."

The view port lightened from complete opacity to a dark neutral tint. Outside the craft lay blue sky and white puffy clouds.

"Looks normal enough," Melanie remarked.

"Famous last words," Jeremy said. "Usually right before the bug-eyed monsters come out of the woodwork."

"Looks like sky," Melanie said, "not woodwork."

"Yeah, well, fine. Okay, Isis, you want to start checking things out?"

"Aye aye, Jeremy dearest. Let me swivel a little."

Isis turned toward the control panel. Jeremy grunted.

"Oh, am I hurting you, dear?"

"Nah, it's fine. Go ahead."

Isis began flipping switches and studying readouts.

"You could probably do this better without virtual body," Jeremy commented.

"Not true, hon. A physical presence gives me an intuitive feel for the physical parameters."

"Oh. Not that I don't like your virtual body."

"I know you do, dear. And I know that you know it's not really all that virtual."

"Uh, yeah. Um."

"Don't be shy." Isis turned her head to Melanie. "He's awfully shy."

Melanie nodded.

Isis resumed her scrutiny of the control panel.

"Shore wish we had our tools," Luster said, "if we're gonna have t' fix 'er agin."

"They would come in handy," Jeremy agreed.

"You can use the tools in the ship's emergency tool kit," Isis said.

"What tool kit is that?" Jeremy asked.

"There is a very small compartment on the port side of the undercarriage, near the secondary positron generator," Isis said. "That's it."

"Is that whut that is?" Luster said, surprised. "Ah opened that up oncet, and there was all these funny-looking rods and things in there."

"Well, they're tools for alien hands," Isis said, continuing to work as she talked. "This ship wasn't built by human beings, you know."

"Wull, ah figgered that's whut they was, but ah don't rightly know iffen we can use 'em."

"Unfortunately, Luster dear, they're all we have to work with."

Lester chuckled. "Wull, in that case, ma'am, ah figger we ain't got no choice but t' try and use 'em."

"That's the spirit, Luster. Oh, dear."

Jeremy said, "What's up?"

Isis clucked and shook her head. "I'm afraid it's a hardware glitch, Jeremy dear. We'll have to put down and make repairs."

"Rats. I hate it when this happens."

"Worse things could happen, Jeremy."

"We didn't even want to go out into the universes. We just wanted to get away from that nut stuff back at the castle. We wouldn't even have—"

"Major malfunction!" Isis was peering intently at a cluster of red lights that had just come on.

Jeremy tried to peer around Isis's head. "What now?"

"Jeremy, honey, we just lost the main graviton flux inducer."

"There's a backup, maybe?"

"Afraid not. This craft never had one installed."

Melanie asked, "What does a graviton flux thingee do?"

The craft began to pitch forward. The horizon crawled up the view port.

"A graviton flux inducer is the thing that generates the antigravity field," Jeremy said. "And that's what keeps the ship up in the air."

Melanie's heart did a flip-flop. "And that means we're going to . . . ?"

"Crash," Jeremy said, scowling. "Boy, I *hate* it when this happens."

KEEP—LOWEST LEVELS

THERE WAS MUCH CLINK AND CLASH of steel against steel in the sitting room—or what was left of the sitting room. The fancy furniture lay overturned. Glass shelves were shattered, their objets d'art strewn over the carpet or smashed against stone. Tapestries lay trampled across the floorboards.

Gene swung mightily, connected, and sent his opponent's banged-up shield flying. Unprotected, the gladiator braced to parry Gene's next assault, but mistook a low feint for the real thing. For a penalty he lost his head, which Gene took off cleanly at the shoulders with one whistling cut.

The severed head left a bloody trail across a Persian throw rug before disappearing.

Gene looked over his shoulder in time to see Snowclaw skewer his adversary, who promptly disappeared.

Linda came out from behind an overturned highboy.

"Yuck! I know they're not real, but I can't stand the gore. I'm getting ill."

"It's not doing my stomach any good, either," Gene said

as he sheathed his weapon, "but the whole phenomenon is getting kind of shaky."

"Meaning what?"

"Meaning these guys didn't have much fight in them. Much weaker than the spooks I first tussled with."

"What do you think's going on? Spell exhaustion?"

"I think that's a good bet."

Linda nodded. "Stands to reason. All this magic, all so overdone. You reach a point of diminishing returns with any spell."

"Right. So maybe the whole shebang will just play itself out?"

"I dunno," Linda said. "A weakened spell can go on for the longest time. It can still be a nuisance."

"I was just hoping we didn't have to go through with this. I'm tired as hell. You tired, Snowy?"

"No. Bored."

"Know what you mean. Okay, you want to try the next level down?"

"Might as well," Linda said.

"Stairs?"

"Let's try an elevator. I think there's a shaft near here."

"Take a shortcut to the source of this nonsense. Right, let's be off."

They walked out of the sitting room and down the hall, threading through a thicket of activity. Variety had begun to evidence itself. The entertainment theme no longer prevailed. Strange and not-so-strange apparitions of many a flavor and stripe came into view. They passed a pair of sailors, a group of women in chadors and veils, several men in conservative suits carrying attaché cases, a motorcycle gang, a man and woman in khakis and pith helmets swishing butterfly nets, a troupe of clowns, six tonsured monks, half-a-dozen state militiamen, an overnight-message delivery woman, several used car salesmen in plaid sports coats, white bucks, and green trousers with white belts, several English bobbies, a tribe of Uzbeks, a gang of stevedores with grappling hooks, a bemedaled officer of the Woman Textile Workers Union of Novocherkassk, a male ballet dancer flouncing about with a nosegay of nasturtiums, a man in a tartan kilt dancing a strathspey, three whirling dervishes, a Maytag repairman, a pride of surgeons in green operating gowns, and a dozen fez-headed Shriners in search of a convention.

These were only the human representatives. Also scurrying about the hallways were orangutans, chimps, gibbons, lemurs, and one gorilla. Flitting through the air came birds of every description, from nuthatches to herons, from waxwings to hummingbirds.

"Hello, hello," Gene said, greeting people amiably.

"Things are getting even more nutsy," Linda said nervously. "Who *are* these people?"

"You got me. Hello, there! Nice day, isn't it?"

A Tibetan monk passed, bowing. Following him was a Jain holy man, stark naked and distributing handbills.

Proffering one he asked, "You read literature?"

"Jain err," Gene told the man, waving him off.

A cloud of multicolored butterflies swarmed overhead. Farther on, black butterflies congregated.

There were a few musicians left. A man bowing a rebec strolled past, followed by a woman playing an oboe d'amore. A small girl blowing an ocarina skipped by.

More animals: two ocelots, three servals, and a small herd of springbok. A pack of Dalmatians ran by, yipping and yelping.

"What weird-looking animals these are," Snowclaw said.

Gene regarded him curiously, but said nothing.

More Dalmatians dashed by.

"This is getting to be Dalmatian Alley," Linda said.

"Good book, terrible movie," Gene said off-handedly.

"Hey, pal, got a light?"

It was a man in historically accurate medieval Hungarian armor, holding an unlit cigarette to his lips.

Gene stopped and searched his pockets. He shook his head.

Linda held out a flaming Zippo. The man lit his cigarette and puffed.

"Thanks," the man said.

"Say," Gene said, "are you in this book?"

"No, I'm just taking a shortcut to the next Steve Brust novel."

"Oh."

The man winked. "See you around."

"So long."

They watched him walk away. Gene said, "Things are getting just a mite screwy here."

"Yeah," Linda said. She stood on tiptoe and peered above heads. "There they are."

A gang of people were waiting for elevators. Gene, Linda, and Snowclaw had to wait ten minutes for the next available one going down. When they boarded, they were surprised to discover a uniformed operator.

"Floor, please?" asked the man in the crisp maroon uniform with yellow piping.

"Basement?" Gene said.

"Basement, Thrift Shop, carpet remnants, step to the rear, please."

They did. "Thrift Shop?" Gene wondered in sotto voce puzzlement.

Linda shrugged.

Two women, decked out in colorful print dresses and expensive jewelry, boarded on the next floor down.

"So I was talking to my daughter-in-law the other day," one of them said.

"The *shiksa?*"

"The blondie. She told me she was going to a flea market next weekend, so I tell her, 'Listen, do me a favor, if you see a used mah-jongg set, I could use one. You know, a nice one with none of the tiles missing. If you should happen to find one, please, maybe, pick it up for me, but only if it's under twenty dollars.' And she says to me, 'What's a mah-jongg set?' Can you believe it?"

The other woman said, "Ciel, listen to me. *Shiksas* in the suburbs don't know from mah-jongg. You know what I'm saying?"

"You're telling me."

"Second floor, notions, mezzanine," the operator announced. The two women got off and several more shoppers boarded, along with a mixture of other types.

The next floor down yielded a motley bunch who began stuffing themselves into the elevator. Gene and Linda were squeezed together up against Snowclaw.

"Oh, by the way," Gene said.

"What?" Linda said.

"I'm going to go out on a limb."

"Oh, you are, eh? How so?"

"Well, I'm going to say something."

"Say it."

"Uh, well, um . . . Linda, I love you."

"You love me?"

"Yeah."

Linda smiled. "Hey, that's great. 'Cause I love you."

"You do?" Gene said, astonished.

"Yup. Do you think we're right for each other?"

"Nope. But what the heck."

"Yeah, what the heck. So, kiss me already."

They kissed. Snowclaw watched with clinical interest.

After a minute or two Snowclaw said, "Excuse me, but what exactly is this thing you're doing? I've never seen you do it before."

"Sorry, Snowy," Linda said, breathless. "It just shows that Gene and I like each other a lot."

"Oh. I get it. But, biting each other like that? Doesn't that hurt?"

"In a way," Gene said.

"Really an odd practice," Snowclaw commented.

"I suppose it is."

"Bargain basement, Thrift Shop, carpet remnants, factory glass outlet! And snack bar. Watch your step!"

A clot of humanity (or a reasonable facsimile thereof) was disgorged from the elevator's open doors. Gene and Linda found themselves carried willy-nilly along with the flow. Snowclaw started shoving hapless individuals out of the way.

"Ease off, Snowy," Gene said.

"Whatever you say, good buddy. Can I bust maybe a few heads, though?"

"No, it's not going to do any good. Just try to keep together."

Nevertheless Snowclaw began to drift away from Gene and Linda, who held each other tight.

Linda gave a painful grunt. "God, we might get crushed to death."

"Well, that's how I always wanted to die."

"How."

"Get mashed to death while making love to a beautiful woman."

"You might get your wish, aside from the beautiful part."

"Nonsense, you're as pretty as they come."

"You'll turn my head, sir, with that . . . uhhh! God damn it, somebody stepped on my toe."

"Kiss me and I'll make it better."

They kissed while the human riptide pulled them across the floor of a vast columned chamber. Linda's feet left the ground. She couldn't get them back down, so she wrapped her legs around Gene. And rather liked it.

"Looks like we're not going to accomplish much down here," Gene said after their lips parted.

"The spell's gone absolutely out of control," Linda said, not really caring all that much.

"We might not make it out of here," Gene told her.

"I know. I love you, Gene, darling."

"I love you, Linda, my love. The only one I ever really loved. Let's have a kid or two."

"Okay, let's."

"Really? I mean, you really think you'd like that?"

"Yup."

"You sure?"

"Actually, I won't know until it happens. They say it hurts like hell."

"Yeah, but the castle midwife must have a spell for that."

"But we might never get the chance to have kids."

"Maybe not."

"Unless I can get these shorts off."

"In the middle of this crowd? Now, that's kinky."

"They're not really people, are they?"

"They're doing a good job faking. Hey, what's this?"

It was a large carved wooden dining table, an island in the middle of a raging sea.

"Push, Linda. Get to it."

"I can't . . . quite get my legs down . . ."

Gene strained heroically, couldn't make headway, then redoubled his effort. Carrying Linda, he broke through the edge of the crowd.

They fell beneath the table. Feet shuffled around them, legs stamped and kicked. But they were safe for the moment. The table was of solid oak and quite massive.

"I want to make an honest woman of you."

"Meaning?"

"A wedding."

"Yes! I love weddings!"

"But shall we, you know, before, do the thing, um . . . ?"

"You mean make love? Of course! I want it."

"I want you, Linda."

"I love you, Gene."

And there, beneath Ervoldt the Third's ceremonial dining table (dating from the first millennium of the castle's history), on a remarkably warm stone floor, they consummated their love while the crowd surged around them, growing ever thicker, and pink giraffes cavorted with black butterflies and golden dragons up among the high, ribbed vaulting.

BELSHAZZAR'S PALACE

THORSBY CAME TO CONSCIOUSNESS feeling nauseated, his stomach burning. He rolled off the divan into a pile of stale half-eaten food and fetid scraps. Holding his throbbing head, he rose shakily. He brushed bits of paté off his toga, then looked about the dais. It was a shambles, strewn with naked bodies, broken bottles, and general detritus.

He looked out across the chamber. There was still a lot going on, but it was all quite strange. He couldn't quite decide what it was he was looking at. Bizarre animals, to be sure, of even stranger hues. Well, they weren't quite animals, were they? After all, animals don't wear seersucker suits—like that orange moose, there. Were those moose antlers? Elk. Well, whatever. And that mauve elephant certainly looked surreal in a kimono.

And what were all these strange creatures doing out there? Some were just milling about. Others sat grouped around card tables. Poker, it looked like. A few bridge games. Yes. Some were just sitting idly by, drinking coffee.

He watched a magenta rhinoceros pour from a silver pot,

filling a mug held by a purple camel in a pink pinstriped suit.

"Say when," the rhinoceros said.

"Whoa, that's plenty," the camel replied.

There was strangeness in the air as well. Hippos like great dirigibles floated above. Lavender, these were, escorted by squadrons of crimson bats. At slightly lower altitudes, vermilion birds soared on rising thermals.

"What in the name of heaven . . . ?"

Suddenly ill, he bent to vomit.

When it had all come up, he staggered back to the divan. On it lay sprawled a houri smoking a cigarette. Her hair was a horror, her makeup streaked.

"What gives?" Thorsby asked.

"What's it look like? I'm bushed."

"I have to sit down," Thorsby said.

"Pull up a wine bottle," the houri sneered. She took a long puff and blew smoke in his direction.

"See here, you cheeky tart—"

"Up yours, dickhead!"

With sudden fury, Thorsby kicked the divan over, spilling the houri into the rubbish. Ignoring the burst of obscenity directed at him, he righted the divan and collapsed onto it.

His tongue, seeming twice as thick as normal, was coated with a velvety, bitter-tasting film. He needed a drink.

"Fetch me a . . . Oh, never mind."

He struggled to his feet and wandered about the dais, rummaging through piles of refuse. He found a half-full bottle and put it to his lips. His eyes bulged. He sprayed the stuff out explosively and dropped the bottle.

"Ye gods, I'm poisoned."

He spat again and again, then wiped his mouth with his forearm. He searched further but came up empty.

The hugely muscled man in baggy pants was sitting on a

corner of the dais, fanning himself with his turban, his legs dangling over the edge. Sweat glistened on his bald pate. His scimitar lay on the platform a short distance away.

"What's going on?" Thorsby wanted to know.

"Not much, pal," the man said sourly as he brought a huge cocoa-colored cigar to his lips. He took a draw.

"But what's all this nonsense?"

The bald man blew smoke away. "Hey, I just work here," he said irritably. "Don't ask me."

Thorsby again viewed the strangeness on the floor below and in the air above.

"Spell exhaustion," he pronounced, nodding confidently.

The bald man gave him a sardonic leer. "You win the door prize, pal."

"About the worse case I've ever seen, too. Balmy, absolutely balmy."

The bald man guffawed. "Look who's talking. The magician who cast the flipping spell in the first place."

"Don't remind me. Gods, what have we done?"

"Ah, forget it. It was fun while it lasted. But it always comes to this."

"Oh, you're at this quite a lot, are you?"

"What are you, a wise guy? We haven't worked in centuries. It just never plays out right, that's all. All we get are jokers like you."

"Well, look," Thorsby said, "if you'd trot out that grimoire and let us have a look at it, perhaps we could fix some things."

"Too late, pal. Can't you see the handwritin' on the wall?"

"The what?"

The bald man pointed toward the far wall of the vast once-sumptuous but now seedy chamber. "There."

Thorsby focused his tired eyes. A disembodied hand was

indeed engaged in an offbeat literary genre—writing, using its index finger as a stylus, on the marble of the pilastered wall. In fact, the hand had been at it for some time. The molding along the ceiling bore this inscription:

MENE MENE TEKEL UPHARSIN

Below it stretched a descending series of tersely wrought sentiments:

MENE MENE MINEY MOE

HEY JERK LOOK UP HERE

THE PARTY'S OVER

EVERYBODY OUT OF THE POOL

YOUR ASS IS GRASS

WARNING WILL ROBINSON!!

HEY STUPID!

WHADDYA GOTTA DO TO GET THIS CLOWN'S ATTENTION?

"Oh, dear," Thorsby said.

"Yeah." The bald man took a long, thoughtful puff on his cigar. "I'd say you'd better vamoose, little buddy. 'Course—"

"What?"

Another long puff. "There's no way outta the joint until the spell completely fizzles."

"What's going to happen to me?"

"You don't wanna know, pal. My advice is, make yourself scarce. When the Grand Wazir makes his appearance, heads are gonna roll."

"The Grand W-w . . . ?" Thorsby swallowed bile. His stomach began its acid churning again.

"Yeah." The bald man sighed. "He don't like bein' toyed with. Know what I mean?"

"I didn't . . . we didn't—" Thorsby suddenly remembered. "Fetchen. Ye gods!"

He began running frantically about the dais, kicking through garbage, overturning bodies, unpiling piles.

"Fetchen! Fetchen, old darling!"

He pawed his way through a mound of rotting beluga caviar.

"Fetchen, speak up, old chap!"

At long last, beneath six layers of unconscious houris, under a mound of rotten fruit and decomposing food mixed with broken bottles and shards of crockery, Fetchen turned up.

Thorsby hauled him out, laid him down, and began slapping his cheeks.

"Fetchen, old chap, come round. That's it, old bean, wake up! Wake up, there's a good fellow."

Fetchen said, "Wuuuuhhhhhhhhhhh." His lips were purple.

"There you go, good as new. Bit of a hangover, eh, old sport? Well, we've all had a bally good laugh, but now it's time to go back to work. Let's be up and doing, come on."

"Uuuuuhhhhhhhhhh," Fetchen replied.

"There we go, there we go,"

"He's had it," came a voice behind Thorsby. It was the bald man, still smoking his noxious cigar.

"No, he hasn't!" Thorsby snapped. "He'll be just as

good as new after I get some coffee in him. You there! Fetch us a cup of coffee!''

''Drop dead, jerkoff.''

''Horrid little strumpet. Smelling salts! Yes, that's what we need. Please, have a little pity.''

The houri chuckled her reply.

''How cruel can you be? This man's dying!''

''My heart's bleedin', honey.''

''You'd let him die?''

''Betcha sweet ass.''

''Better it happens now,'' the bald man said, turning away.

KEEP—HIGHER UP

PEOPLE EVERYWHERE!

Throngs of them, droves of them. People of every description decked out in every sort of wild get-up. Kwip had never seen so many different varieties of human creature. And they were all after his loot!

"That's mine!" Kwip screamed at the man with the odd pill-shaped cap.

"How do you figure, mate?"

Kwip grabbed at the sparkling sapphire ring. When the lanky sailor held it out of reach over his head, grinning, Kwip let him have a boot in the groin. The sailor went down and Kwip had his ring back. The encircling crowd voiced its disapproval, hissing and booing.

"To the devil with all of you," Kwip snarled as he ran off, the bulky sack of recovered booty rattling against his back.

First endless musicians, then big cats, then gladiators, and now this. He'd nearly lost his life to the cats—that last pair had chased him down six flights of stairs—but Kwip almost preferred them to this horde of sticky-fingered scavengers.

Through a chink in the rush he spied a gold chalice lying on the stone floor of the corridor; but he wasn't quick enough. Before he could reach it, the thing got kicked. It skittered down the hall and ended up being punted into a side passage.

Hefting the overstuffed sack, Kwip pushed and shoved his way after it, but the press got ever greater. Someone stepped on his toe and he yelped. Then someone trod on his heels; he let loose a punch to the kidney in answer. The man on the receiving end collapsed against his neighbor, who in turn tripped up two unfortunate passers-by, who . . . and so forth. This domino effect generated a minor tussle, which Kwip struggled to get away from.

At a safe distance, he resumed the pursuit. Drat. Now he'd lost sight of the chalice. He stooped and peered among the hosts of stamping feet, and for his trouble got goosed up the backside. He clouted the nearest suspect, who was in fact completely innocent; but no matter. Kwip ducked the retaliatory blow, which landed on another bystander, who became justly aggrieved—and in no time a major brawl broke out between a construction gang and some gentlemen in leather vests and odd helmets.

Kwip couldn't slip away from this quarrel. A giant of a man came at him and he had to resort to whacking the brute with the sack, which promptly split open.

A cascade of baubles and bangles splashed to the floor: bracelets, anklets, earrings, and chains; pins, brooches, chatelaines, torques. Out gushed gems and precious stones of every sort and value: diamonds, emeralds, agate, and heliotrope, onyx and amethyst, all clattering and tinkling and skittering into every nook and corner.

There ensued a mad scramble for the scattered treasure. Fist fights broke out all over. Shouts and curses. Fingers gouged at eyeballs, knees found their way to sensitive parts. Elbows jabbed into solar plexuses.

At length Kwip crawled out of the swirling maelstrom. He got to his feet, saw a swinging door, and fled through it.

He found himself on a wide landing between stairways with a high Palladian window, overlooking courtyards far below, set into the far wall. Amazing to behold, there was no traffic on the stairs. Kwip sat himself down on the stone window seat and burst into tears.

All his swag, gone. How many years' work? Half a dozen, at least. Piles of pretty gewgaws, heaps of fancy trinkets, gold, silver, and platinum gimcracks. All lovely little bijous, and all irretrievably lost. Washed away like sand castles with the rising tide.

Castles! He never wanted to see the inside of another castle as long as he lived. He would hie himself out of this insane place once and for all. He would choose a likely looking aspect, one of tidy villages peopled by sturdy upright middle-class stock, prosperous burghers, every man, woman, and child. And he'd steal them blind and live at his ease and be happy forevermore.

He let loose a great despairing sigh. Gods. No, truth to tell, he'd probably stay here. Stealing was work, and Kwip had never cared much for work. Which was why he stole in the first place. In the past few years he'd slacked off something awful. He liked to steal, he loved his profession, but when there was no real need for it . . .

Ah, well.

The door on the landing burst open. Kwip looked up and was puzzled when no one came through. The door eased shut. He shrugged and went back to brooding.

"Kwip."

Kwip was startled to hear a disembodied voice at his side.

He jumped to his feet and searched about, yet still saw no one.

It is I, Osmirik.

Kwip said warily, "Where are you?"

In front of you. One moment.

Kwip was astounded when Osmirik materialized before his eyes.

"Sorcery, is it?" Kwip asked.

"Of a low sort," Osmirik said. "With it I avoided the sword fights, but these teeming multitudes make passage through the castle impossible." He cast glances up and down the stairwell. "Seems to be thin in here."

"Aye. But I hear rumblings below."

Osmirik listened. Sounds of mounting feet drifted up from the depths of the stairwell. His shoulders fell.

"The way is by no means clear," he said.

"By no means," Kwip agreed. "But then, why descend to the lower floors? Thence come all our troubles, me-thinks."

"True, but I must get to the source, which, I have surmised, may be a certain hidden storeroom in the crypt."

"Think you?"

"Indeed. I may be able to abrogate the spell, or at least inform the king so that he may do so."

"Aye, good. But getting there's the rub."

"True."

Osmirik sat and thought.

Lord Peter Thaxton came running down the stairs and skidded to a stop on sight of the two dispirited men.

Thaxton was breathing hard. "What gives?"

"Nary a thing," Kwip said. "I've just lost my life's fortune."

"Just lost my best friend," Thaxton said.

Osmirik was about to ask who, but realized it could only be one man. "My condolences. How came it about?"

"Details later, please," Thaxton said as he sat down heavily. "Must get my second wind."

"We are essaying to find a way to the lower keep," Osmirik said.

"Me, too," Thaxton said. "If there's a chance he may be alive, I've got to get to him."

"I see."

"Besides, I've got to alert the Guards, all that," Thaxton said, then bent over and put his head between his knees. "Sorry, bit dizzy."

"Rest awhile, my friend," Osmirik bade him. "Meantime, I shall think."

"Bloody hell," Thaxton said, for no particular reason.

"Aye." Kwip concurred in this sentiment.

"Bloody awful," Thaxton said. "Nasty business."

Kwip nodded in baleful agreement. "Aye, it is."

Thaxton lifted his head. "You saw it, then?"

"I was there," Kwip said.

"You were? I didn't see you."

Kwip came out of his wistful reverie. "Pardon? What say you?"

"I said, if you were there, I certainly didn't see you. Whereabouts—?"

"I've got it!" Osmirik shouted, jumping to his feet.

"What's that?" Thaxton said.

"The way down. Help me open these casements."

Thaxton and Kwip exchanged doubtful looks, but assisted Osmirik in unlatching the windows and swinging them open. Outside was a narrow ledge. Osmirik stepped up onto it.

"Just what do you have in mind?" Thaxton wanted to know.

"We shall jump."

Thaxton looked at Kwip, then at Osmirik. He turned away, reaching back to massage the nape of his neck. "Everyone's gone balmy," he muttered.

Kwip scowled at the Royal Librarian. "Ye gods, man, have you lost your senses? Or is this more sorcery?"

"None of my doing. You do know that the castle is tricked out with many spells?"

Kwip snorted. "Hardly a revelation."

"But did you know that there is a spell, a series of them, which can catch a man if he fall from a great height?"

"You're daft."

"Hardly. No one can fall to his death from Perilous as long as these spells are efficaciously operative."

Thaxton, at first dumbfounded, managed to say, "Good God, man. Are you quite serious?"

"As long as the spells are working. We can jump safely to the ground and—"

"Wait just a moment," Thaxton said as he bounded up to the ledge. "If a man fell off the highest part of the castle, from the highest parapet, are you telling me that there's a chance he could survive?"

"Why, yes," Osmirik said. "If the spell on that part of the castle were still effectively running. One such spell cannot cover the whole castle, and they do fail now and then—"

"But is there a chance he might survive such a fall?"

"Why, yes, that's exactly what I am saying, Lord Peter. And we have that same chance. If we can but screw our courage to the sticking point—"

"Ta ta!" Thaxton said happily as he jumped from the ledge.

"Gods!"

Osmirik watched him drop. Astonished, Kwip leaned out

of the window and witnessed with him. Neither could quite believe his eyes.

"Why . . . it works," Osmirik said in awe.

"I'll be buggered six ways from Whitsuntide."

"Well," Osmirik said. "We shall meet below. I hope." Osmirik jumped.

Kwip watched again. He still could not fathom it.

"I do believe something strange is going on here," said a voice behind him. Kwip whirled about.

And there stood a giant rabbit. The thing was about seventeen hands tall from its huge feet to the tips of its long ears. The fur was a bright hot pink where not covered by a morning coat and ascot, pinstriped pants, and spats. No shoes. The rabbit was smoking a meerschaum pipe.

"So," the rabbit said, puffing philosophically. "Doing a little Zen skydiving, eh?"

Kwip's eyes widened to saucer-size. He turned and dove out the window.

ANOTHER WORLD

The *Sidewise Voyager* plunged, if not earthward, then other-worldward.

As calmly as possible, Melanie asked, "Uh, Jeremy? Is there anything we can do?"

"Well, we can always go back into non-space," Jeremy said.

Sitting on Jeremy's lap, Isis shook her head.

"O'course," Jeremy went on, "that's no solution. We can't stay there indefinitely. But with no antigrav we can't land anywhere to fix anything. So we're kinda stuck."

Melanie looked through the view port. The ground was coming up frighteningly fast.

"Uh, maybe we'd better do something, like, soon?"

"But if we spend any more time in non-space," Jeremy said, "the ship's hull will take a beating. It can only handle so much stress. What we should do is maybe try a shuffle."

"A shuffle?"

Isis said, "We send the craft on a tangential course, touching each universe in succession but not really entering except for the briefest nanosecond. But that presents another problem.''

"Yeah, we get even loster that way," Jeremy said.

"Well, technically that's not true," Isis said. "Without a functioning nav system, we're lost, period. It's just that we could shuffle forever, trying to luck into the castle's universe.''

Melanie watched as the ground raced upward at an alarming rate. She said, "Uh, people, I suggest we do something, anything, *right now*.''

Jeremy said, "Huh? Oh, yeah." He reached and flipped a switch.

The view port went completely blank. Outside was nothing but an indeterminate grayness. Non-space; nothingness; nowhere.

Melanie let out a sigh of relief.

"I guess we can stay in non-space long enough to set up a shuffle," Jeremy said. "If we should want to do one.''

"Definitely not," Isis said.

"You don't think so?"

"No. We should try to jury-rig a software patch.''

"Yeah? How?"

"We use the schematics on board to simulate a nav unit.''

Jeremy brightened. "Hey, that's an idea. But how do we calibrate it?''

"By using the readings that are in the storage buffer.''

"Might work," Jeremy said. "Might work. But . . . hmmm.''

"Objections?"

"Well, the time factor, for one.''

"Good point," Isis said. "But I have a plan. We shuffle until we find an empty universe or one with no planetary masses nearby. We'll be in zero-g, but we can manage.''

Jeremy shook his head. "I dunno. First of all . . . wait

a minute. Doesn't this ship always drop in near a planetary mass because it sniffs out big masses in non-space first?''

"Exactly. So we'll have to override.''

"Boy, that'll take even more time.''

"Certainly. But we have no choice. Of course, we have the option of dropping in and out of non-space.''

"That's too risky, and besides we can't do much with the ship systems when we need 'em to fly.''

"True again.''

"But I don't like—'' Jeremy glanced at the control panel. "Oops, better get back into normal space before we get squished.''

"Squished?'' Melanie said.

Jeremy looked at her. "Yeah, the pressure could flatten us like an aluminum beer can.''

The sky—or another one—appeared again, and again the ship began to nose over and dive for the ground. To Melanie the experience was beginning to seem like being trapped on an endless roller coaster ride. Her stomach did a flip-flop.

Jeremy and Isis debated again while the ship dove. Melanie waited as long as she could stand it, then shouted a warning. Jeremy responded, sending the ship back into non-space. Jeremy and his "assistant'' then carried on the technical discussion until it became time to dump back into normal space. And the horrifying cycle began over again.

Melanie couldn't bear it.

"Jeremy,'' she said. "Do something.''

"Huh?''

"*Do* something. Get us back home. I don't care how you do it.''

"Hey, we're trying, Melanie.''

"You're not trying hard enough. If this up and down stuff goes on any longer, I'm going to puke all over the compartment.''

"Don't get it on the controls, please!"

"Jeremy, it's going to go all over the place. I'm sick, Jeremy. It's coming up. I can feel it."

Jeremy made a face. "Oh, God, please don't. I can't stand it when that happens. Makes me wanna puke, too."

"Then *do* something, Jeremy. You're supposed to be a genius."

"Wait, I have an idea," Isis said. "Jeremy, you were taking readings on the location of the magical disturbance shortly before you took the ship out, weren't you?"

"Yeah, why?"

"Why don't we use the ship's sensors to detect the spell from non-space? That would give us the vector parameters for home, wouldn't it?"

Jeremy snapped his fingers. "It would if you recorded the readings for me to calibrate the sensors with."

Isis smiled. "I did, Jeremy. I automatically record everything you do at the work station. The buffer has it all."

"Great! Isis, I love you."

"Jeremy, darling!"

The two embraced as the ground rushed up yet again.

Melanie screamed, "We are going to *fucking crash* if you people don't get on the stick!"

"Sorry!" Isis said and swiveled toward the control panel. She hit the thruster just in the nick of time. The *Voyager* slipped back into the temporary safety of non-space.

Melanie nearly fainted.

"One thing," Jeremy said. "Those coordinates, the ones pinpointing the disturbance, could be anywhere in the castle. We'll materialize there. It could be a broom closet, for all we know. We have enough trouble landing in the graving dock, which is, like, huge."

"We will be cutting it very close, Jeremy dear. But if we get our entry velocity down as close to zero as we possibly can, we'll have a very good chance of making it with minimum casualties.''

"That's going to take some fancy math," Jeremy said.

"Math is our business," Isis said brightly. "Now, dear, let's get to work. We have only forty-five seconds left before we have to dip back into normal space again.''

"Right. Boost your clock speed to five hundred mega-hertz.''

"Done, dearest Jeremy.''

Melanie rolled her eyes. *Minimum casualties.* Wonderful.

Suddenly realizing that the Gooch brothers hadn't uttered a peep in some time, Melanie looked back.

They were fast asleep.

BAY SHORE

THE STRAND WAS DESERTED. The great ships were gone, but men had left their signs everywhere. Here a sandal, there a piece of armor; elsewhere a broken blade, already painted in verdigris, a blue-green shard in the sand. There were other things: abandoned fire pits; discarded articles of clothing, sun-bleached rags. More, much more. The shore was littered with refuse.

He walked by the edge of the water, snorting and sniffing. The water smelled fishy, brackish. He climbed a dune and bent to nibble beach grass. It was salty, otherwise tasteless. There was not much to eat and he was hungry. Sand flies tickled him, and he swished his tail absently.

The day had dawned clear. There had been no men about since the night before. They were all gone. He did not miss them much.

Not at all, in fact.

But now he again heard the voices of men. He turned his maned head to look.

Two men approached. They looked not unlike the other men, but wore different dress. More colorful.

"What a beauty this one is!"

"A white stallion, like the others. Why do you think they left them?"

"Who knows? Why did they leave so suddenly?"

"We beat them off, that's why! Here now, fellow. Easy, easy."

One of them petted him. He didn't quite like that. But he let a looped rope be put over his head and around his neck.

"Easy, boy. Gods, what a horse! Spirited, but well-broken. Perfect."

"Big one. Too big for the saddle I've got."

"Oh? So, you won't mind if I take him."

"What? I saw him first."

"You just said your saddle isn't big enough."

"To hell with that. He's mine."

"Here, now. There may be others."

"Or there may not be. He's mine, I tell you."

"Shove off."

"You shove off! Oh, so it's going to be that way, eh?"

"You don't want to go up against me."

"Don't make me laugh. I'll slit you from gills to gullet before you can—"

"*Hold off, you two!*"

Another man, this one shorter but with a voice that seemed to carry more authority.

"Sheathe those swords! Now!"

"Yes, sir."

"Where did this one come from?"

"Just wandering about like the others, sir."

"A fine specimen. The best of the lot. I'll relieve you of it, subaltern."

Reluctantly, "Yes, sir. Very good, sir."

"What a magnificent horse! A gift of the gods, in honor of our victory. It must be so."

"Very likely, sir."

"Yes, yes. The Arkadians wouldn't have left anything so beautiful, so valuable."

The new man slapped his rump.

"The Arkadians didn't have much to leave behind, did they, boy? Except their dead." He laughed. "And now, with their war chests depleted, we'll take to raiding their coasts and plundering their towns at our leisure. Won't we, boy?"

Another slap on the rump, another burst of laughter.

Weasel.

"You two take the other horses back. Put them in the palace stable."

"Not in your personal stable, sir?"

"Don't be absurd. All these animals are the property of His Majesty. Now, do as I tell you. I'll take this one to the palace myself."

"Yes, sir."

The first two left. The one remaining stroked his neck lovingly.

"Yes, you'll stay in the royal stables, but you're mine. I'll ride you down the main street of Mykos. You'll have new armor, burnished like the sun, and a new war mantle. No dragging chariots for you, my fine fellow. I'll be sitting on you when we watch them lop off old Anthaemion's head."

He was led away.

Yeah, right. You don't know it, pal, but you are going to get yours. Tonight.

The stables smelled bad but he didn't mind so much. The hay was good, what little there was of it. At midday, oats was served. It was tasty. But as the day wore on, the stable hands seemed to slack off. They missed the evening feed altogether. They were falling-down drunk by then.

There was much jubilation in the city. Voices were raised in triumphant shouts. He heard singing, much singing, heard crowds move about. He saw women run by; then, men running after them with hungry smiles on their faces.

Night fell, and the celebration went on. The citadel rang with laughter and song. A thousand lamps blazed up on the acropolis, where choruses sang hymns of thanks to the gods. Elsewhere there was feasting and drinking. Much drinking. Bonfires lit up the night.

There was a bay roan filly at the other end of the stable. She smelled good to him and he wanted to get to know her.

But there was work to do. Later. Later that night. Besides, he must remember who he was and what he was.

The dead of night arrived. The city was quiet. Voices had stilled and the fires were embers now and all the lamps had gone out on the acropolis.

A dog barked, far away. A wind had come up, sounding over the unmanned walls of the citadel. Most of the lookouts had drunk themselves into a stupor. Most of the city's soldiery were sprawled in their wives' or lovers' beds, or in the stables, or in the gutter.

It was time to remember that he was not what he seemed to be, though it was a very difficult thing to accept. It seemed that he had always been like this. This was a natural state of being for him. There were no concerns, there was no worrying. It was easy to be this way. He rather liked it.

But he knew, he knew. He was not a horse. He was a man. And it was time to stop being a horse. To do that, he had only to want to be a man again.

Did he want to be a man again?

Yes. So . . .

Now.

He was down on his hands and knees in the stall, naked. The floor reeked of dung.

"Yuck."

He got up, bent to gather straw, and cleaned himself. Then he looked about. No one. Nothing was stirring. He wondered where Telamon was, and if his magical transformation had reversed yet.

He moved cautiously out of the stall, unlatching the gate carefully. He looked up and down the mews. It was dark and he heard not a sound.

He walked from stall to stall, searching for white stallions. He saw horses, but none white.

He came to a seemingly empty stall and looked in.

His servant Strephon rose from a crouch out of the darkness.

"It is I, master."

"Where's Telamon?"

"I saw him. He is looking for you."

"Go find him, bring him here."

"Yes, master."

Strephon walked off into the darkness of the stable. Very soon he returned with two men. Trent smiled at Telamon and his servant Ion.

Trent asked, "Where are the other two?"

"Still in their stalls, waiting."

"Send Ion to get them. They've reverted, haven't they?"

"Yes. I think we all reverted on schedule. You are a brilliant sorcerer, my friend. I really, truly was a horse. I saw the world as a horse sees it. It was . . . strange. Yet absolutely marvelous."

Trent nodding, smiling. "It is an amazing experience. You get the idea that it might be better to be an animal rather than a human."

"Yes. Remarkable. Go, Ion. Fetch the others."

Ion stole away into the gloom.

"What now?" Telamon said. "Can we find weapons?"

"Easily, though we mustn't be seen by anyone who is still awake. I saw enough passed-out troopers out in the mews to accommodate us all. We strip them and take their weapons. And then move down the hill, quietly, quickly, and take the north tower. From the sound of things out there, I'd be surprised if we found one sober Troadean."

"I also heard a lot of commotion earlier. Drunken revelry."

"After two years of hard siege, for it suddenly to be lifted would give one cause to celebrate."

"Indeed," Telamon said.

"But we have to move silently and quickly. Not everyone is unconscious, surely, and there might be one or two guards who take their jobs seriously."

"Understood. Here are the others. They know what to do."

"Okay." Trent counted. "All six accounted for. We pair up and go out and forage, then report back here when we have weapons. Clothes are optional. We don't really need them to do our work. If the man you're rolling shows any sign of coming to, kill him quickly and silently. Understood?"

"Understood."

"Above all, make no noise."

"Also understood."

"Telamon, you take Ion. I'll take Strephon. You and you are a team. Okay, is everybody ready?"

Nods.

"Right," Trent said. "Telly, you first. I'll wait sixty beats of the heart before I send the next team out. Okay, go!"

Ion and Telamon left.

"Strangest thing, I was beginning to feel like Mr. Ed, there, for a while."

"Master?"

"Never mind."

The streets were dark and quiet. The wind had grown gusty, its dull roar making it all the more easy to make their way through the city with complete stealth. Following twisted streets, they came down from the acropolis with its grand palace and its temples, into the city proper.

Silence ruled. Windows were dark. Not even an alley cat made an appearance to mark their passing until they got to the poorer sections of town. They heard voices and dispersed into the shadows.

Two drunken soldiers were escorting a drunken woman between them. The three weaved down the street and negotiated the next corner.

Trent watched them. The woman shrieked once, far off. Whether a belly laugh or a cry of dismay, he couldn't tell.

It became quiet again. Trent signaled Telamon, and the commando team resumed their mission.

Troas was small, no more than five hundred yards in circumference. A legend even in its own time, it was nonetheless little more than a fortress. They reached the north circuit of the outer wall in short order.

Trent surveyed the battlement from the shadows. Nothing seemed to be stirring above. If lookouts had been posted they were not manning their positions.

He had expected the city to let its guard down, but the extent to which this had occurred was surprising. Had everyone in the place swilled themselves into oblivion? In and around the stables the soldiers they'd rolled hadn't moved a muscle. It had been like undressing manikins. Trent was sure one man had been dead: alcohol poisoning, heart attack, or he'd choked on his own vomitus.

Was everyone in town completely smashed, passed out? Well, they'd soon find out at the high watchtower, the one that guarded the northern gate of Troas.

Those legendary topless towers. Trent regretted mightily having to burn them. But when Anthaemion's lookouts saw the signal fire Trent's men would set, the Arkadians would return in force, in the middle of the night. Trent would then open the main gate of the city and let them in.

And then the bloodshed would begin. The slaughter. The Troadeans wouldn't have a chance. The Arkadians, maddened by two long frustrating years of stalemate, would give no quarter. No mercy. They'd easily kill all the males of military age, probably males of every age, including infants, especially the children of nobility. They'd rape most if not all the women, then carry them off as concubines, servants, and slaves.

And when they'd done all that, when the slaughter and plundering and looting were done, they'd put Troas to the torch.

The sack of Troas.

Damn. Trent did not want to do this. But he had to. He'd given his word.

He gave the signal to move in. Telamon sprinted across the street and flattened himself against the base of the tower. Ion followed.

The honor of opening the door devolved to Trent. It was

secured from the inside, of course. Secured very early this evening. But Trent had it open in a trice with a simple door-opening charm. There was no lock; the massive oak door was barred with a heavy wooden beam which a bit of levitation took care of handily (after Trent had used his clairvoyant powers to see behind the door).

They slipped into the tower and closed and barred the door after them. It was pitch-dark inside, save for the light spilling through tiny embrasures on every floor. They climbed the narrow stairs single-file.

It happened on the fourth level. The stairway was blocked; with what, Trent could not see. It felt like a stack of crates or trunks. Puzzled, he reached behind him, took Ion's hand, waited for him to link with the others, and led into the adjacent chamber.

They were suddenly jumped, and a fight in total darkness ensued. Before he could begin to draw his sword, Trent had several sets of hands laid on him. He kicked out but didn't connect. In answer, a solid clout to the head knocked him down.

Light blossomed. A beam of light stabbed his eyes.

A *flashlight* beam?

He heard a familiar chuckle. Three Troadean soldiers had him pinned. The fight was already over, his commando teammates all subdued.

"Who the devil are you?" Trent said to the man holding the flashlight.

The man turned the beam upward to illuminate his own smiling face.

"*Inky!*"

Incarnadine's apartment in the palace was luxurious.

"How long have you been mage to the court of Troas?" Trent asked as he stuffed himself with a very late supper. He had to admit the fare was better than the oats and timothy he'd enjoyed earlier. Actually, it was good to be human again.

"Oh, many years, local time," Incarnadine said, sipping the same dark, sweet wine Trent was drinking. "In fact, I wormed my way into Mykosian culture chiefly for the purpose of saving Troas, my favorite city here."

"Tell me again why you used me as a cat's-paw. My head's a little thick tonight."

"I couldn't very well be in two places at once," Incarnadine answered. "I needed someone convincingly good as a strategist, yet someone whose mind I knew well and could second-guess. I couldn't let you in on my plans because Anthaemion surely would have sensed your duplicity. He's as cagey as they come, and a bit of a telepath."

Trent nodded. "Okay, I buy that. I had enough trouble with him. Despite my best efforts, he seemed to sense that I disliked him and that I was half-hoping that the whole operation would fail. How did you know I'd try the Trojan horse bit?"

"I didn't, but I was prepared for one sort of commando operation or another, and knew you'd be trying to take the watchtower at the north gate. The horse-transformation thing was a brilliant stroke, Trent. Masterly bit of deception. I think they would have chopped up the wooden version for firewood, it's so scarce around here."

"Right. But it's strange how the horse motif persists."

"I've followed the Troy thread in over a dozen worlds so far. It's the central legend in dozens more. Something basic is at the core of it, but I don't know what, yet. One of the things I'm studying. But all the versions I've encountered are the same in essentials."

Trent looked out the window, west, toward the sea. The city was still dark, but daybreak was not far off.

"Anthaemion's out there, somewhere, waiting for my signal fire."

Incarnadine nodded. "And when rosy-figured dawn breaks without his having seen anything, he's off for home, never to return. And Troas is saved."

"And a legend is lost. You're right, this mythos is central to most Earthlike cultures. What cultural havoc are you wreaking here?"

Incarnadine chuckled and pushed a scroll across the table.

"Scan that."

Trent unscrolled what looked like the beginning of a long poem written on sheepskin.

"'Sing, Muse, of the wrath of Aeakides . . . '" Trent gave his brother a sardonic look. "What, you joined the Blind Poets' Guild?"

Incarnadine laughed. "No, but this culture will have its heritage. As is true in most worlds, later generations will never be sure of the historicity of any of this. But they will have the poem. As for Troy—or Troas—the bay will silt up, the citadel will lose its strategic value, and it will eventually be abandoned."

Done eating, Trent sat back and drank off the rest of his wine.

"Nevertheless, my dear brother, I am mightily pissed off at you."

Incarnadine shrugged. "I can well understand."

"Why didn't you let me get word to Sheila, for gods' sake? I can't believe your insensitivity. You know how she—"

"There is no need to."

"What? What the hell are you talking about?"

"The time difference between the castle and this world is variable. I couldn't tell exactly how long you'd be gone, castle time. I knew it would be short, but I didn't figure on how short. The slippage factor shot up to five digits and has remained so the whole time we were here."

"Five digits? You mean we've been here over two years, and only—"

Incarnadine nodded, grinning. "Only a few hours have passed back at the castle."

Trent was struck dumb.

Incarnadine chuckled again. "So when you get back it'll be late evening of the day you left. Remember that when you see Sheila."

Trent laughed in spite of himself. "You rotten, no good . . ."

"Sorry. But she'll never know, unless you choose to tell her."

"Are you kidding? I wouldn't . . . Hold it, hold it. You're forgetting we have to get back to Mykos to go through the portal."

"It was originally here. I moved it back."

"Oh."

"So everything's fine."

"Whoa, just a another minute now. This doesn't let you off the hook, my friend. You *duped* me."

Incarnadine nodded. "That I did. Rather well, too."

"Artfully. I'm going to get back at you."

"I'm rather sure you will. Have some more wine." Incarnadine reached for the pitcher.

"Thanks."

"By the way, something's been happening at the castle while we've been gone. I'm getting vague vibrations, but I'm sure it's some sort of strange magic."

Trent didn't answer immediately. Then he said, "It will be long in coming, and when it comes it will be sudden, unexpected, and frightful."

"All good revenge schemes should work that way," Incarnadine said, pouring. "Say when."

CRYPT

"ARE YOU SLEEPING?"

"Hm? Just have my eyes closed."

"This floor should be hard and cold but it's not cold at all. It's not exactly soft, but it's not exactly uncomfortable either. What do you think?"

"Hm?"

"Do most men always sleep after?"

"Ah, the perennial question of male post-coital somnolence."

"Huh?"

"We should get up. By the way, notice anything?"

"Yes. Everything's quiet. No crowds, no nothing."

"Yeah. Did you notice when, in the middle of everything, it got awfully strange? I mean, intensely strange?"

"Yeah, I saw weird feet. Big pink bunny-rabbit feet."

"Yeah, and chartreuse elephant feet, and like that."

"Right."

"And then, very suddenly, everything got wispy and faded out."

"Right. I noticed. I was rather preoccupied at the time, of course."

"Of course. Me, too. Let's get out from under the table."

They crawled out and dressed hurriedly.

The huge underground crypt was empty except for a few curious pink clouds scudding near the ceiling. They seemed to emanate from the crypt next door, and toward this destination they began to walk.

"Are we near the source, do you think?" Linda asked.

"I'd venture to say that we are," Gene said. "But the source seems to have dried up."

"Thank God. Is it over?"

"The weirdness? Don't know. Hope so."

They passed through a tall arch that followed a corbeled passageway which made several L's. After the last one, a short walk brought them out into another huge crypt, but this one was strange. It looked like the interior of an ancient ruin. Its marble walls were cracked and pitted; decorative friezes lay in shards along the floor. They passed dry fountains and stands of dead potted palms. Debris littered the floor.

The place was deserted except for three people up on a platform at the far end of the hall, toward which Gene and Linda moved.

Pink and purple clouds drifted amongst the tops of high columns. Here and there a Day-Glo butterfly flitted and fluttered.

"Hello?" Gene called as he began mounting the stairs to the platform.

"Hello," came the reply.

Gene and Linda reached the top of the stairs and looked around curiously. The place was an ungodly mess.

"Hello, there. I'm Thorsby. This is Fetchen."

Gene asked, "Is he all right?"

"Uhhh," Fetchen answered.

"He'll pull through," Thorsby said. "Thought I'd lost him, but he's doing fine."

"Good," Gene said. "Let me ask you a question."

"Fire away, sir."

"What the hell has been going on here?"

"Ah! Yes, of course, you would want to know that. Well, that's going to take some explaining. If you'd just give me a minute to collect my thoughts. Been in a bit of a dust-up, don't you know. Almost didn't pull through myself. We've had no end of trouble, no end of trouble."

"They had one hell of a good time," said the large bald man who sat at the far end of the dais.

"Who's that?" Gene asked of Thorsby.

"Uh. Actually, I don't know. I say . . . sir? Do you have a name?"

"Just call me Omar."

"Omar, I'd like you to meet"—Thorsby turned to Gene—"I do know your name, sir, but it escapes me at the moment."

"Gene Ferraro. You're one of the apprentice magicians, no?"

"Right you are, sir."

"So you two are the jokers who cast the wild spell?"

Omar laughed. "Oh, did they screw it up."

"Well, now, we certainly did achieve some spectacular effects."

Omar hooted.

"Yeah, I'll say you did," Gene admitted. "Did you know you about had this castle in the worst uproar it's ever been in?"

"Did we know? Oh, no, sir, we did not. Did . . . uh, did some of the manifestations escape?"

It was Gene and Linda's turn to laugh.

"Our apologies for any disturbance we've caused," Thorsby said. "But I assure you that it was all quite inadvertent. The unfortunate result of a series of thaumaturgical accidents, which, as I'm sure you understand, are sometimes unavoidable when one engages in important scientific—"

"*Ah-hah!*"

Gene and Linda turned and saw no one, though the voice had come from behind. Linda gave a squeal when she bumped into a dark-bearded man in turban and slippers who was not quite three feet tall. He wore colorful silk robes and several emerald rings. Despite his size, he looked like trouble.

The dwarf turned his head to Omar. "Are these the two?"

"That's them, boss."

The dwarf swiveled his gimlet gaze to Thorsby and Fetchen. "You incompetent, lazy, stupid, miserable good-for-nothings have succeeded in queering my karma for the next six hundred cycles of existence."

"See here," Thorsby said. "Who the devil are you?"

"You're talking to the Grand Wazir, boys," Omar told them.

"Oh. Uhhhh . . ."

Fetchen picked that moment to sit up. He blinked his eyes and said, "I'm feeling much better." His eyes focused on the Wazir. "Hello. What are you?"

The Wazir's dark bushy eyebrows lowered. "What am I? I'm the canker on your gum. I'm the boil on your bottom. I'm the worst nightmare you ever sweated through. That's what I am, you contemptible, scrofulous, illegitimate get of a diseased, flea-bitten camel."

Fetchen turned to his mate. "Who's this little wanker, then?"

"Yes," Thorsby said indignantly. "Get along with you, tiny person, before you get hurt underfoot."

The Wazir howled and charged.

He was on them like a swarm of gnats. There seemed to be dozens of him, all kicking shins, biting fingers, goosing bottoms, and elbowing crotches. Thorsby and Fetchen ran from the chamber screaming, pursued by a miniature whirlwind of nastiness.

When they had gone, Gene and Linda burst into helpless laughter.

As they were recovering, Omar stood and stamped his cigar out. He yawned.

"Well, I'm off. Nice meeting you people."

"Same here, Omar," Gene said. "Where exactly are you going?"

"Back into the woodwork. I'll be on unemployment for the next millennium, probably." He sighed. "Ah, well. So long."

He walked down the steps and headed off into the gloom that lay between two columns.

They watched him fade into darkness.

Gene looked at Linda. "Feel kind of sorry for him."

"Me, too."

"Say, woman. You and me have some wedding plans to discuss."

"Yup. Church or secular?"

"Oh, church. We have that huge chapel upstairs."

"Great! I'd never figured you for a church-wedding type."

"Me?" Gene said. "Why, I'm as pious as they come."

"Oh, yeah."

Just then, Cleve Dalton came walking into the crypt.

"Cleve!"

"Halloo!"

After Dalton mounted the stairs he felt the need to sit, and the one intact divan was all there was to sit on, which he did, despite its being a filthy mess.

"Is it all clear upstairs?" Gene asked.

"All clear," Dalton said. "It was over pretty quick. Everything just started to fade, and then it all went *poof*, like that. Nothing left but some pretty smoke." Dalton sized up the place. "Looks like someone threw a hell of a party down here."

"Yup. By the way, Linda and I would like you to be the first to know that we're—"

"There you are, Dalton."

Lord Peter Thaxton came sprinting up the stairs. "Well, you look hale and hearty."

"No problem," Dalton said. "Something tells me you found out about the safety-net spell."

"Firsthand. You must have had a ghastly time of it, though, not knowing."

"I dunno. It was one of those experiences that you are grateful for afterward and hope never to repeat."

"Indeed." Thaxton turned to Gene and Linda. "And how about you two? What did you do during the brouhaha?"

"Oh, we—" Gene began.

Linda covered his mouth. "We hid out with Snowclaw." They looked at each other.

"Snowclaw!" was their duet of dismay.

"Yo!" came a voice from the rear of the chamber. Snowclaw came forth, gnawing on a curious object. It looked like . . .

"Ohmygawd, a pink bunny leg," Linda said, making a face. "I think I'm gonna be sick."

"Funny thing," Snowclaw said, climbing the steps. "I can't even taste this. It's like fluff."

By the time he reached the top of the stairs all that

remained was the yellow spat that had wrapped the foot. Snowclaw tossed it aside.

More people entered the hall: Deena, Barnaby, Du-Quesne, Sheila, Kwip, Osmirik, and lots more. Everyone wanted to see what had caused all the ruckus.

But there was more ruckus to come, because at that moment a strange bell-shaped silver craft materialized out of thin air and promptly crashed into the far wall.

"We keep doing this," Jeremy mumbled as they pulled him from the wreckage.

Miraculously—and this is meant quite literally—all the occupants were only slightly injured. The craft had been outfitted with technological magic, and a protection spell had absorbed most of the shock. (Or was it a force field? No matter.)

"Come on, Dolbert," Luster said. "We got to start fixing this blamed thing again."

Dolbert snickered. Then he yawned. He'd had a restful nap.

Melanie emerged with only bruised knees and a sprained arm.

"Nice little trip."

"By the way, where are your kids?" Deena asked.

"Safe with my babysitter, away from the castle. Which is where I'm heading, right now. Sometimes this place gets too much for me."

"Oh, you love it here," Gene taunted.

"Yeah, I know. I must be crazy."

"Aren't we all?"

And as far as this narrator has been able to ascertain, they all live there still, quite happily, and will doubtless continue to do so ever after.